AFRICAN ADVENTURES

Stubby Stories No. 2

By

Lloyd Fezler

MASTER BOOK PUBLISHERS
SAN DIEGO, CALIFORNIA
92115

African Adventures
(Stubby Stories No. 2)

Copyright © 1984

MASTER BOOK PUBLISHERS, A Division of CLP
P. O. Box 15908
San Diego, California 92115

Library of Congress Catalog Card Number 84-60869
ISBN 0-89051-099-7

Cataloging in Publication Data

Fezler, Lloyd 1918-
   African Adventures.

   (Stubby Stories Adventures, No. 2)
   Title.
                                  813
ISBN 0-89051-099-7   84-60869

Cover by Colonnade Graphics, El Cajon, CA

Printed in the United States of America

About the Author

Dr. Lloyd LeRoy Fezler was born in Osakis, Minnesota. He spent his childhood, youth, and adolescence in that small rural town. His memories of that community, nestled on the shore of a beautiful lake, are impregnated with fondness.

The late high school years of his life were filled with dreams that encompassed being a "big league" baseball player, but these dreams were never fulfilled. Days prior to graduation from high school, a severe injury brought him to death's door. His dreams were shattered by the effects.

After a two-year recovery period, his family encouraged him to pursue a teaching career. Four years later he received a Bachelor of Science degree, with majors in science and social studies. The teaching of science (biology, chemistry, and physics) became his speciality.

While his children were young, the Stubby Stories came into existence. They were originated while Dr. Fezler was away attending summer school. The first twenty-one stories ("Adventures at Mountain Haven") were designed for his two youngest children.

As time passed, Dr. Fezler was selected to go to Africa as a member of the Teacher Education Program in East Africa. For three years he was stationed in Kenya. There he became acquainted with the life patterns of several species of wild animals. Thousands of pictures were taken.

Two years after returning to the United States, he was selected to go to Thailand. It was while living in

Bangkok that the "African Adventures" were written for three young ladies who became his godchildren. It is to these children, godchildren, and "son" Walter that the stories are primarily dedicated, with a feeling of deep appreciation for the beauty given to life.

The author extends a special thanks to Mr. Meeker and his family for their encouragement, to Dr. Henry Morris for introducing the stories to the publisher, and to JoJo for her inspiration.

It is Dr. Fezler's greatest desire that "tiny" Stubby will help someone find a "big" love for Lord Jesus.

Prelude

Bright sunshine filled the morning sky making the flowers, trees, and grasses sparkle as its rays of light bounced off the dew drops that covered them. Yes, it was a beautiful day, but Mr. Stubby Stevens made it a day that I shall always remember.

When I first met Stubby, he was 21 years old. He came to stand beside me while we waited at a bus stop. As he looked up at me, I saw his blue eyes and pleasant smile. He was a good looking young man, but he was so small. When he sat beside me on the bus, his feet didn't even touch the floor.

Later, as I came to know this little man, I found out that Stubby did not know his real parents. As a tiny baby he had been left on the doorstep of Mr. and Mrs. Stevens. When they were unable to find his parents, they adopted him. As foster parents, they cared for him and loved him as he became a fine young man.

After Stubby graduated from high school, he took special training as a welder, as an electrician, and as a mechanic. He became a skilled worker.

We rode the bus until it stopped at an aircraft factory where I was "boss." At the gate leading into the factory, the guards glanced at my pass and I entered, but Stubby didn't have a pass so he was stopped.

As I walked toward the company offices, I heard the little man say, "I came to see Mr. Clark. I didn't make an appointment, but I really want to see him."

I turned around. The guard looked at me and grinned as I walked back to the entrance gate.

"Young man," I said, "I am Mr. Clark. What do you want?"

Stubby smiled, "Mr. Clark, I want to work in your factory. Look at me. I am so small that I can crawl into places easily that big people would have a tough time reaching. I'm a good welder, electrician, and mechanic. Besides these things, I am willing to work hard."

I took Mr. Stubby Stevens into the factory with me and hired him. He turned out to be an excellent worker who had many good ideas. His job was to help build airplanes and helicopters.

When Stubby became 42 years old, he decided to retire. He had completed 20 years of work at the factory. Everyone who worked with him, and there were more than 2,000 workers, knew and loved him.

As a goodbye present, we decided to give him a helicopter. Stubby already knew how to fly a 'copter, so it was an excellent gift. The little man liked it very much.

Helicopters have other names. At the factory, they are called whirlybirds, 'copters, and choppers.

Stubby's helicopter had special steps, seats, and equipment because he had such short arms and legs, so he had no trouble flying it.

Have I ever told you the height of this little man? Why don't you get a meter stick? A meter stick is just about right. Stubby is 39½ inches tall, but he really is a little "giant" of a man in everything he does.

How tall are you? I'll bet almost all who read about Stubby stand taller than this little man, but you must remember, Stubby is a midget. He will always be a tiny man.

Chapter One

The months of planning were ended. Everything was ready. The two little men were about to begin their trip to East Africa. It had been decided that they would spend most of their time visiting and traveling in Kenya. Only short trips would be made into the East African countries of Tanzania and Uganda.

At one time, Kenya was a British colony, so many of the black people had learned to speak English. Of course, they spoke their own tribal language as well.

Because Kenya is famous for its wildlife, it is a country visited by many tourists. As they traveled in Kenya, Stubby and Bobby hoped to see herds of zebras, elephants, wildebeests, hartebeests, elands, gazelles, giraffes, oryx, and other strange animals.

Stubby said, "If we are lucky, we may even see lions, leopards, baboons, monkeys, and lots of things. We may even see cheetahs, although there are not many of them left." Of course, the two little travelers expected to see many kinds of birds, snakes, and bugs, as well as trees, plants, and flowers.

While planning their visit to Kenya, the two little men had learned the word "safari." It is an African word, and it means "trip." Stubby and Bobby were going on a safari, but the boy traveler still thought the whole idea was a dream.

On the day the safari was to begin, Stubby awakened early. Even the sun was still hiding behind the mountains when the little man opened his eyes. Stubby's son was also hiding, but Bobby was hiding under the blankets on his bed. The tiny boy was hiding and snoring.

Stubby's eyes sparkled with love for Bobby, then he gently shook the young boy. "Wake up, Son," he said, "You can't sleep all day. Come on get out of bed. It is time to rise and shine."

Bobby sat up in bed. Although he was still almost asleep, he said, "Let's go, Dad. We can skip breakfast. I'm not hungry. Let's go."

Stubby laughed. Bobby wasn't even dressed. He hadn't taken his shower, brushed his teeth, combed his hair, or anything, but it made Stubby happy to see how excited Bobby was about visiting Africa.

It was only a few minutes after Bobby got out of bed that the sun poked its round head above the mountains. Stubby looked at the beautifully colored mountains and forest. He thought, "My son Bobby and the sun in the sky both belong to God. He takes care of them while they both brighten my life. What a wonderful God."

The clock was about ready to strike seven times when a car drove into the yard at Mountain Haven. A married couple got out of the car. Their names were Max and Sue. Stubby had asked them to stay at Mountain Haven while he and Bobby were gone. Max, with Sue's help, would take care of the ponies and fill the bird feeders. Mostly they would just enjoy the wildlife that visited the Haven.

Max and Sue had two young daughters. Stubby loved them almost as if they were his own children.

The little man knew the young girls would really like seeing all the forest birds, animals, and flowers. Like their mother and dad, the two girls walked with God. They could see the beauty of His creations.

A few hours after his friends arrived, the two travelers climbed into the helicopter. The 'copter would take them to the airport in Seattle. Stubby said, "Bobby, I hope you have a wonderful safari."

He smiled at Bobby and then started the whirlybird. As Bobby shouted, "Africa, here we come!" the helicopter slowly rose from the ground.

The whirling blades of the 'copter turned faster and faster as the helicopter climbed into the sky.

Tears filled Bobby's eyes as he looked down at Mountain Haven. He would really miss his wildlife friends. He would especially miss Silver Tip and the ponies.

The chopper circled the farm, but it did not head for Seattle. Bobby asked, "Where are we going? Aren't we going the wrong way?"

Stubby laughed. He said, "No, I am not lost. Seattle is not this way. Do you remember the stream and waterfall where we camped? I mean the waterfall where we met Fantail. Well, Silver Tip likes to fish in that stream. If we fly to the stream, I hoped maybe we could see him. Maybe we can wave goodbye to him. Yes, I know it sounds 'goofy' when I mention waving goodbye to a bear, but I still like my idea."

It didn't take long to fly to the waterfall. Minutes later, when Bobby looked out the 'copter's window and saw the falls, he almost cried. Why? It was because the sun's rays were reflected by the falling water. The reflected rays made a beautiful rainbow.

The picture was very beautiful to see. It made him
feel lonesome although he had barely begun the
safari.

Stubby flew the helicopter in a big circle above
the stream. He lifted his hand and pointed his
finger.

When Bobby looked where Stubby pointed, he
saw Silver Tip. The big bear was wading in the
stream. Tip was fishing.

Silver Tip looked up. When he saw the
helicopter, he stood on his back legs and waved
with his front feet.

Bobby said, "I know he is only doing what you
taught him, but he sure looks as if he were waving
to us."

Silver Tip's front paws were going up and down.
The two little men waved to Tip. Stubby laughed.
He said, "I am glad that no one can see us. I am
sure that if anyone were watching, they would think
we were crazy. Normal people don't fly around in
a helicopter so they can wave goodbye to a bear,
but who ever said we little people were normal."

After another circle above the stream, Stubby
turned the chopper and headed toward Seattle.

Suddenly, he leaned forward in his seat. The little
pilot looked toward the edge of the forest. He said,
"Can you see those two men? What are they
doing?"

When Bobby spotted the two men, they were
standing in the trees near the forest's edge. The
men carried rifles. "I think," he said, "those men
are hunters! They must be after Silver Tip! They
will kill him! Dad, we have to help!"

Stubby picked up his microphone for the radio.
He called the park rangers. He asked the rangers to

come to the waterfall. Rangers, as you know, help protect our wildlife. He said, "Hunters are after a grizzly bear. They are in a protected area. Please come quickly. It isn't even hunting season."

The rangers grabbed their guns. They didn't even wait for Stubby to finish talking, but ran to their helicopter right away. Very quickly, their whirlybird took off and headed for the waterfall.

The little chopper pilot hung up the microphone. He looked down. The hunters were crawling closer to Silver Tip. Very soon they would be ready to shoot the bear.

Stubby said, "We'd better get down there in a hurry. Help is coming, but I don't think the rangers will get here until it is too late." The little pilot dropped the helicopter toward the ground. The 'copter fell almost as if it were a rock.

Will the rangers get to the waterfall in time? Will they be too late to save Tip?

The tiny pilot was going to land the whirlybird right between the bear and the hunters. Just before the chopper landed, Stubby held the helicopter a few feet above the ground. He used the whirling blades to blow dust all over the hunters. The dust even got in the hunters' eyes. A moment later, Stubby landed the 'copter. He landed at the edge of the stream. At once Stubby climbed out.

When the hunters saw Stubby, they shouted with much anger in their voices. "Get out of our way! We want that big grizzly bear! Move out!"

In a calm voice, Stubby spoke. "The rangers," he said, "are on the way. I called them on my radio. It is not legal to hunt in this protected area, and it is not even hunting season. If you can see the bear, you will see that he is wearing a chain collar. His

name is Silver Tip. He is my friend. I will not let
you kill him."

While Stubby was speaking, Silver Tip waded out
of the stream. As he stood shaking water from his
hair, he was hidden by the helicopter. When he
finished shaking himself, the great grizzly shuffled
along behind the helicopter. He was right behind
Stubby when he came around in front of the
whirlybird.

One hunter shouted, "Look out! The grizzly is
right behind you." He raised his gun. He was ready
to shoot Silver Tip, but Stubby was in the way.

Quickly, Stubby raised his hands. He shouted, "I
told you the bear is my friend. Put your guns
down!"

Bobby jumped out of the helicopter. He ran to
Tip's side. The tiny boy hugged the big bear. It was
a real bear hug.

Silver Tip walked up behind Stubby and pushed
him with his nose. Stubby said, "Why don't you put
down your guns? Silver Tip is so close to you that
if I commanded him to charge, he would probably
kill both of you even if you shot him. Would you
really want to kill him? Isn't he a special bear?"

The hunters were scared. They lowered their
rifles. They also backed up. It was easy to tell that
they didn't really believe what their eyes were
seeing. A hunter said, "Am I really seeing two little
people playing with a giant grizzly bear? I'll never
be able to tell my friends. They will all say I'm not
telling the truth."

Bobby smiled. He said, "Dad, let's really give
them something to talk about. Let's show them a
few things that Tip can do."

Stubby had Silver Tip do several tricks. The big

bear even stood on his back legs and danced. Finally, Bobby said, "Tip, lie down." While the bear was resting, the two little men climbed on his back. When the boy said, "Up, Tip," the big bear got to his feet. He carried Stubby and Bobby wherever they told him to go.

Watching the two little men and the giant bear was much like going to a circus. The hunters began to laugh and clap their hands. Wow! They really did have a story to tell their friends, but I do not think many people would believe them.

Another helicopter came over the mountains. It landed right next to Stubby's 'copter. Two rangers jumped out of the chopper. When their feet touched the ground, the rangers seemed to freeze.

As they landed, they had seen a big grizzly bear stretched out on the ground. Through the helicopter windows, they had seen Stubby and Bobby sitting on the big bear. Of course, they thought the bear was dead. Silver Tip didn't even move when the rangers landed their 'copter.

When they jumped out of the helicopter, they were very close to the little men and Tip. Their guns were still in the helicopter. Stubby and Bobby stood up to shake hands with the rangers. At that moment, Silver Tip also stood up. It scared the rangers so much that they couldn't move or speak.

Stubby said, "Don't be afraid. Silver Tip will not hurt you. He does everything I tell him. You are not in any danger."

The rangers breathed deeply. A ranger said, "I have heard wild stories about two little men and a grizzly bear, but I laughed at them. I'll certainly never laugh again."

When the rangers turned to the hunters, they

were angry. The hunters lost their guns and received big fines to pay. Because Silver Tip was not killed, the hunters did not have to spend time in jail.

The rangers promised Stubby that they would check on Silver Tip while the little men traveled to Africa.

Pilot Stubby and co-pilot Bobby climbed into their helicopter. They said goodbye and headed for Seattle.

Bobby said, "We almost lost Silver Tip. Those hunters were really going to kill him."

Stubby smiled. "Son," he said, "remember, God even watches over the sparrows."

Chapter Two

It was early in the afternoon, when Stubby and Bobby landed their helicopter at the Seattle airport. Mr. Clark and Tom were there to meet them and to help the two little men carry their bags.

People stared at the midgets as they walked through the air terminal. A few of them laughed at the two little men.

Bobby had tears in his eyes. He was sad because people were laughing at him.

Mr. Clark saw the tears. He said, "Bobby, do not feel sad. Just try to be as tall as your Dad. Son, your Dad is the tallest man I have ever known. He stands far above most people. Do you understand?"

A smile came to Bobby's face. "I guess," he said, "you are saying I don't have to *be* tall to *stand* tall."

Mr. Clark grinned. "Remember, Bobby, your Dad stands at least ten feet tall. You will soon see."

The four men reached the waiting area. The area was crowded with people. There was no place for the friends to sit down. All of a sudden, at least 25 people in one group stood up. They turned to face Stubby, Bobby, and the Clarks.

One man, who was taller and stronger than the others, picked Stubby up. He held him high in the air, then he gently stood him on the floor. He said, "Hi, Partner. I sure do miss you at the factory. We

all miss you. When Mr. Clark told us you were
going on a trip, we decided to take a day off. It is
great to see you, my dear friend."

Stubby's friends crowded around him. They shook
his hand. Some picked him up, but they all wished
for him to have a wonderful trip.

A man, who had laughed, said to his friend,
"Wow, he must be famous."

Mr. Clark heard the man speak. He said, "Mister,
that little man is a child of the King. I, personally,
owe my life to him. All who learn to know him
always end up loving him. He is Mr. Stubby
Stevens."

An announcement came over the loud speaker
system. It was time for Bobby and Stubby to get
on their airplane flight to Minneapolis.
At the departure gate, sometimes called the
goodbye gate, Tom Clark lifted Bobby up. Tom
gave him a big squeeze, then he whispered into his
tiny ear. "Goodbye, little brother," he said, "I love
you."

This made Bobby very happy. He gave Tom a
big hug. "Tom," he said, "you are my big brother,
but Dad says, in God's eyes...we are all brothers.
Big or small, short or tall, no matter what color our
skin might be...Jesus loves us."

Tom Clark would never forget what Bobby said
to him.

Stubby and Bobby walked up a ramp and
entered a big jetliner. Only a few minutes later, the
jet thundered down the runway and roared into the
sky.

This was Bobby's first ride on an airliner. The
young boy kept looking out the window. First, he
watched the trees, buildings, and ground disappear,

then the jet plane became surrounded by clouds.
After a few minutes, the jet climbed above the
white misty blanket. Now he could look down on
the white tops of the cloud blanket.

"Dad," Bobby said, "does God come way up
here? I'm kind of scared."

Stubby answered. "God," he said, "is everywhere.
I don't know how God does it, but I know that it is
true. God is with us all the time. His Word tells us
He is."

In Bobby's thoughts, the airplane trip had just
begun, but a sign told him to fasten his seat belt.
The jet was on its way down for a landing. It
wasn't long before it landed in Minneapolis.

At the Minneapolis stop, Stubby's old teacher got
on the plane. Now Bobby would get to meet the
man about whom Stubby had told him so very
much.

Both little men watched for the gray-haired man.
Finally he came walking down the aisle and stood
beside Stubby. After the tiny traveler had talked
briefly with his old teacher, Stubby turned around.
"Bobby," he said, "I would like you to meet my
old teacher and friend. This man, we all called him
'Doc,' was my high school science teacher. As you
know, he lived and worked in Kenya for three
years. We will be together in East Africa, and he
has volunteered to be our personal guide. Doc, this
is my son, Bobby."

Doc said, "I am pleased to meet you. If you are
like this man called Stubby, you are part of the
very best."

Stubby whispered, "It was Doc," he said, "who
taught me about Jesus. I owe him very much. He
loved me when I thought no one could love a

midget. He insisted that I was taller than most big people. He gave me strength when I needed it the most. He is a dear friend."

When Bobby looked at Doc, he saw the silver-gray hair that covered his temples and the smile wrinkles on his face. In Doc's eyes Bobby saw warmth, understanding, and love. There was a sparkle that made the boy happy.

The jet plane zoomed through the sky. After a brief stop in London, it headed for Kenya. Bobby was so excited. He could hardly wait for the jetliner to land in Nairobi. When the jet did land, he could hardly wait to get off.

A few minutes after the landing, Bobby, Stubby, and Doc were on the stairway that led to the airport's waiting room. Suddenly, Bobby stopped. He stared at the people. All of them had black or dark brown faces. The faces seemed to be staring at him. He was afraid!

An African errand boy for the airlines stepped forward. He smiled, then he spoke. "Jambo," he said, "welcome to Kenya." Bobby grinned at the black lad. Doc had already told him that "jambo" means hello. The tiny white boy's fear ran away.

Bobby said, "Dad, I think that boy wants to be my friend."

Immediately, Doc bent down. He whispered, "Bobby, you must remember never to call a black Kenyan a 'boy.' 'Boy' is a bad word to the black people of Kenya. Do you know why?"

Bobby shook his head. He was a boy, and it did not anger him to be called a boy. Why should it make black Kenyans angry?

Doc explained. "Kenya was at one time a British colony. Africans were servants and the British called them boys. When orders were given, it was 'boy do this' or 'boy don't do that.' Even men were called boys."

Bobby listened. He was beginning to understand.

Doc continued. "When Kenya won its freedom, the blacks were no longer forced to be servants. They became free. They do not like to be reminded of the years under the British. Calling them boys is an insult. They are proud, free men."

Bobby understood.

As the men entered the airport terminal, a brown man grabbed one of Doc's bags and ran down a hallway. Bobby shouted, "He is stealing Doc's bag! Stop him!"

The man was sure to get away. The three friends could not run fast enough to catch him. He would be lost in the crowd at the waiting gate.

Just as he entered the crowd, a slender African grabbed him. He held the brown man tightly until Doc, Bobby, and Stubby came puffing to his side. When the black African grabbed the brown African man, the brown man dropped Doc's bag. Strangely, Doc handed the man a dollar and thanked him for carrying his bag. The brown man said, "Thank you, sir. Thank you for saving my honor. I shall be grateful to you forever."

After the brown man had disappeared into the crowd, Doc slowly turned around. He put his arms around the slender black African. Tears were in his eyes as he squeezed the African. The gray-haired man seemed to be crying and joyful at the same time. He said, "Jambo rafiki. God bless you."

Finally, Doc turned to Bobby and Stubby. "This man," he said, "is Abdi. He is my very dear friend. He has always been near when I needed him to help me."

Doc turned to face Abdi. "Abdi," he said, "this is Stubby and his son, Bobby. Stubby was once a student of mine. We thank you, rafiki, for coming to meet us. You have greatly honored us."

Bobby noticed that when Abdi smiled the African's teeth were almost all gold. It gave him a friendly look.

Abdi extended his hand toward Stubby. The black man said, "Jambo rafiki or should I say, hello friend." The two men shook hands. A new friendship had been born.

The black Kenyan with Doc at his side and followed by Bobby and Stubby made his way through the crowd of people. He took the three men to a Land Rover. All four men climbed into the Rover. Doc sat up front with Abdi, while Bobby and Stubby sat in the back seat. Abdi drove his friends to his home on the edge of the Nairobi National Reserve.

Bobby asked, "What is a reserve?"

Stubby answered, "A reserve is like a big farm. Wild animals live on reserves and hunters are not allowed to shoot them. It is an area protected by rangers. Abdi and his rangers are the protectors of the wild animals that live on the Nairobi National Reserve."

It was night when the four men got to Abdi's home. When they entered the house, Doc spoke. "Abdi," he said, "we are very honored to be guests in your home. We will try to make you proud."

Not long after arriving at Abdi's home, the tired visitors and Abdi went to bed. Bobby, Stubby, and Doc spoke to Jesus, then they went to sleep.

Warden Abdi was the first to awaken when

morning came. As soon as his eyes were open, he rolled out of bed, dressed quietly, and then went outside. The black Kenyan stood on the porch listening to the early morning sounds.

Abdi tipped his head to one side and listened intently. The warden heard an animal coughing. The sound was far away and it barely reached Abdi's ears.

Quietly the African went back inside. He tiptoed into Doc's room. The gray-haired man was out of bed. He was kneeling. Doc was saying his prayers. Abdi waited. When prayer had ended, he spoke softly to Doc.

"Doc," he said, "listen. Do you hear that coughing sound? It is a long ways away, but I think we can find it. Shall we try?"

Doc listened. He could hardly hear the sound. He smiled at Abdi. "Yes," he said, "I think we all should have a look."

Quickly, Doc entered Stubby's room. He awakened both little men, but he spoke to Bobby. "Young man," he said, "if you ever get out of bed, Abdi will take us into the bush country."

Bobby bounced out of bed. Doc laughed heartily. "Slow down," he said, "at that speed your motor will burn up."

The four men had an early breakfast. When they were finished, Abdi led the way to his Land Rover and the four friends climbed inside.

As Stubby got into the back seat, he stopped. "Gee, this is great. It will be easy to see. . .even for little guys like Bobby and me."

Warden Abdi had placed another car seat on top of the Rover's seat. Its purpose was to lift the little men higher.

Abdi backed the Rover out of the driveway. He headed toward the animal making the coughing sound. As they bounced across the bush country, the Warden spoke, "Do you hear well? Have you got good ears? I'm going to stop for a minute. I want you to listen, then tell me what you hear."

The Rover stopped. Four small ears listened. They heard the coughing sound. Bobby said, "I hear a coughing sound. Whatever it is, it surely has a bad cold."

Once again the Land Rover bounced across the bush country. At times, Abdi stopped the Rover. He listened to the coughing sound. Each time the sound seemed to be closer. The black man was pleased. He was sure that he could find the animal making the sound.

Chapter Three

Bobby and Stubby did not like the coughing sound, because there seemed to be anger present.

The Land Rover rumbled across the bush country of Kenya. It pushed its way through the tall grasses and bushes heading straight into the breeze. The Rover bounced along as its riders searched for an animal that was making a coughing sound.

Bobby and Stubby sat on the "high seat" Abdi had fixed for them. The seat was in the back of Abdi's Land Rover. From their high seat, the two little men stared out of the Rover's windows. As they bounced along, Bobby turned to look at his Dad. Finally, he reached out and touched him. When touched Stubby turned to look at his son. Bobby whispered, "What are we looking for?"

Stubby answered, "I don't know for sure, but I think it is a . . . ."

The Land Rover changed its direction. It made a sharp turn to the left. It turned so quickly, Bobby and Stubby almost fell off the seat. A few seconds later, Abdi pushed hard on the brake. The Rover skidded to a quick stop. This time both the little men, who were riding on the high seat, fell "kaplunk" on the floor.

As Bobby and Stubby scrambled back onto the seat, Abdi said, "Look over there." The black man pointed to something in front of the Rover.

Bobby and Stubby looked out the front window.
They looked where Abdi's finger pointed. The two
little men smiled. What they were looking at surely
wasn't going to go away, at least not very fast, but
why had Abdi stopped so quickly?

As they looked out the front windows, they
could see the golden rays of the rising sun
spreading across the grasslands and painting the
hillsides. The Ngong Hills had crowns of gold.
Stubby sighed, "It is a beautiful sunrise. Thank you
Abdi, for stopping."
Abdi chuckled. He said, "I do not mean the sunrise.
I want you to see what is hiding in that tall grass."

Very quickly, Bobby slid across the seat. He
squeezed against Stubby. The eyes of the two little
men almost popped out. Tiny Bobby was afraid. He
was shaking.

Just a short ways from the Land Rover, almost
completely hidden by tall grass, the four men were
able to see a big brown and tan animal. Although
the animal was hard to see as it lay hidden in the
grass, even Bobby knew it was a lion.

This was the first lion Bobby had ever seen,
except for those on TV and in the movies, or at the
zoo. Stubby's son whispered. "Wow, that is surely a
big cat. Aren't we too close? I can count her
whiskers."

Abdi whispered, "Be very quiet. Now turn your
heads slowly to the right. A zebra herd is coming
our way. If you make any quick moves, you will
probably frighten them away."

The African was looking out a window on the
driver's side of the Rover. It was a window on the
right side of the four-wheel-drive Land Rover. Of
course, you probably didn't know that drivers sit on

Abdi whispered, "Be very quiet. Now turn your heads slowly to the right. A zebra herd is coming our way. If you make any quick moves, you will probably frighten them away."

the right side in Kenya, while in America drivers sit on the left. Bobby, Stubby, and Doc turned very slowly. They looked out the windows on Abdi's side. At first, all they saw was one zebra. The zebra limped as it came across the grasslands. It was limping toward the tall grass where the big cat lay hidden. A moment later, far behind the lone zebra, the four friends spotted several more zebras. The zebra herd was following the low zebra.

Doc had a name for the lone zebra. He called him, Old Stripes. Old Stripes was the herd leader. He was leading his herd to a water hole. The zebra herd was following the lone zebra.

The zebra leader was a stallion. As you know, something was wrong with the leader. He limped badly. Even from their seats in the Rover, the friends could see that the leg of Old Stripes was badly swollen. While the men sat watching, the male zebra stopped and stretched out his left front leg. The stallion bit at his ankle.

Doc whispered, "Stripes' leg must be hurting badly. It is badly swollen. I wonder if it is a snake bite?"

When the leader stopped to bite his ankle, the whole herd stopped. Near the edge of the herd, a young zebra flopped to the ground and rested almost under its mother's feet. A short distance away, another young zebra stood by its mother's side.

Bobby said, "Baby stripes has brown stripes. Why are they brown?"

Stubby answered, "Brown stripes make the young zebra harder to see when it stands in tall grass or bushes. It is God's way of helping protect them." When Stubby finished, Old Stripes started limping along once again.

The zebra herd leader moved closer to the water hole. He also moved closer to the long grass where the big cat lay hidden.

The zebra stallion's nose smelled the breeze, but the breeze was blowing away from Old Stripes. It was blowing in the wrong direction, so it did not warn the herd leader. It did not tell him that a lion was waiting near the water hole.

Cautiously, Old Stripes moved forward. His eyes looked into every shadow and his ears listened to every sound as he limped along. The zebra leader did not see, hear, or smell the big brown cat.

Once again, the stallion leader stopped. He turned his head. Old Stripes seemed to be staring right at the hidden cat. Suddenly, the zebra leader screamed loudly. He whirled around. Quickly, he started to run away, but his hurt leg was weak. Twice, it made him stumble. Although the herd leader did not fall, the hurt leg kept him from running very fast.

When the zebra screamed, the big brown cat jumped out of the tall grass and raced rapidly across the bush country. Very quickly, she caught up with Old Stripes. In one long jump, the big cat landed on the zebra's back. Her long teeth bit into the neck of the stumbling stallion. Old Stripes squealed only once, then he fell to the ground.

Old Stripes, the zebra herd leader, was dead. The brown and tan cat had made a "kill."

Tears filled Bobby's eyes. He sobbed, "Why didn't we warn him? We could have tooted the horn. If we had just yelled out the Rover's window, Old Stripes could have run away."

Doc reached back and squeezed Bobby's knee.

"Young man," he said, "we eat several kinds of animals. It seems to be part of God's Plan. Some animals have to die so that other animals can live. This lioness was probably....'' He did not finish speaking. The lioness roared so loudly, it even scared Doc. Of course, little Bobby almost hid under the back seat.

Only a few seconds passed, then Bobby peeked out the car's windows. "Wow," he said, "look at those pointed teeth."

The lioness had her mouth open. She was ready to roar again, and her long teeth were easily seen. Bobby whispered, "Now I know she could bite me to pieces. I'm sure glad that I'm not her breakfast."

"That lioness," Abdi said, "has probably been hunting most of the night. Lions rarely make a kill unless they are hungry. She would die if she could not find food. I will bet that she has babies, and her cubs must have food. She is trying to be a good mother."

Stubby whispered. He said, "Look behind the Rover. Here comes a whole bunch of lions. I count five cubs and another lioness. Am I right?"

His friends nodded their heads. The little man was right. The lions walked past the Land Rover so it was easy to count them. In fact, if mother had not been there, Bobby could have reached out and touched a lion cub. And remember, Bobby's arms are not very long.

Just before it reached the dead zebra, one of the cubs stopped. It turned its head and looked at the men in the Land Rover. When the cub faced Bobby, it was like a big kitten. Bobby's sadness went away and he thought, "Of course, cubs have to have food. It must be part of God's Plan just like Doc told me."

The lioness who had killed the zebra licked the faces of three cubs. She was their mother. Even the lionesses greeted one another in a very friendly manner. After saying hello, the seven lions began to eat.

Doc said, "Everything is well planned. One lioness hunts, the other lioness babysits. Young cubs have to be protected. God's Plan is good."

While Bobby, Stubby, and Doc had been talking, Abdi had looked at the zebra with his binoculars. He asked Stubby and Bobby a question. "Did you see Old Stripes stumble?"

The two little men nodded. The African kept speaking. "It is true," he said, "that a lioness needs food. She needs food to keep her alive and to feed her cubs. Old Stripes might have died even if he had not stumbled, but I think his hurt leg helped the lioness to catch him. We will drive closer as soon as the mothers have full stomachs. I want you to see what was wrong with Old Stripes' leg. You must see what made him limp."

While the lions were still busy eating, Abdi drove closer to the dead zebra. No one in the Land Rover spoke. When they were very close to the "kill," Abdi whispered. The little men could barely hear him when he said, "Look at the left ankle. Can you see it? Can you see the band of twisted wire? It is pulled so tightly around the leg of Old Stripes that his blood could not move. That band of twisted wire is a snare trap. It gets so tight that the animal's blood cannot flow. If the blood cannot flow, it causes a kind of poisoning called gangrene. If Old Stripes had not been killed quickly by the lioness, he would have died slowly and painfully from the poison. Who really killed the zebra? The poachers who set the snare trap really helped."

Doc said, "Lots of troubles are caused by poachers. Somehow, we must stop these illegal hunters. We have to stop them or our wildlife will soon be gone. Legal hunting may be all right, but poaching is wrong."

Stubby told his son more about poachers. These bad hunters usually use snare traps to catch big cats. Old Stripes was probably caught by accident. The trappers/poachers, were probably trying to catch a lion, leopard, or a cheetah.

"It could have been worse," Stubby said. "There are still quite a few zebras, but some of the big cats are almost all gone."

Three of the men in the Rover gave thanks to God. It truly could have been worse. The four friends sat until lunch time watching the lions eat, then they drove into the shade of an acacia tree. Stubby served lunch. It was sandwiches, ice-cold pop, pickles, potato chips, and for dessert—a fresh banana.

Bobby laughed. "In Africa, I eat picnic lunches in the car. It is fun, but I would not like to eat inside if I were back home."

After lunch was finished, Abdi drove from one ranger station to another. He asked two important questions at each station. First, have any poachers been reported? Second, have the cheetahs been seen? The answer was the same for both questions. The rangers said, "No!"

Another day was ending. Bobby yawned, "Gee, it gets dark early. It seems as if I just got out of bed." He yawned again.

Stubby smiled. "Son," he said, I think your yawn

machine is telling you that it is later than you think. A big yawn like yours means sleep time is almost here."

Darkness covered the bush country. If the men could have seen in the dark, they could have seen a leopard creeping up on a sleeping gazelle and three lionesses moving quietly through the tall grasses as they "stalked" a wildebeest. Another lioness waited in the bushes. Seven cubs were at her side. This lioness was the babysitter for the three hunters.

Leopards and lions often make their kills when the light of day is dim. These big cats are sometimes called "silent killers."

Chapter Four

At the break of dawn, Stubby, Bobby, Abdi, and Doc had everything loaded in the Land Rover. The friends were going back to the place where the lioness had killed Old Stripes.

When the Rover stopped beside the zebra carcass, the lioness, her lady friend, and their five cubs had stuffed stomachs. Some of the cubs had moved away from the dead zebra. The three cubs who were babies of the lioness that killed the zebra herd leader curled up in a shaded place. One cub lifted its head and stared at the four men, then it stuck out its tongue.

Bobby laughed. He thought lion cubs were much like baby kittens. He scratched his head. Would a lion cub be a good pet? The tiny boy was not sure.

One of the mother lions finished eating, then she stood up. Slowly, the lioness strolled into the shade of a tree and stretched out on the grass. Mama lion was ready to take a nap.

Very slowly, or as Abdi would say in Swahili "poly poly," the black African drove the Rover close to the resting lioness. In fact, he drove so close that Bobby could easily count her whiskers.

When Bobby took a good look at the lioness, he said, "No, no, no...I do not want a lion cub for a pet. I almost forgot that nice little cubs grow up. They also grow long pointed teeth and strong sharp claws. Nope, I do not want a lion for a pet."

As the men sat watching the lions, another lion gave a rumbling roar. The lion was right alongside the Land Rover, and the roaring made everyone in the Rover almost jump right off their seats.

The heads of the four men turned quickly. Four pairs of eyes looked out the Rover's windows. What they saw was a good reason for jumping.

Only a few feet away from the Rover, there was a big male lion. This male "simba" stood straight and tall. His head was held high. Doc said, "Stand still please, Mr. Simba." He grabbed his camera to take a picture.

Bobby and Stubby slid across the Land Rover's seat. They moved as far away from the lion as they could go. Stubby whispered, "Simba means lion. It is a Swahili word."

Abdi grabbed his hunting rifle. The African spoke softly to Bobby and Stubby. He said, "It is the lion we call Scarface. He is probably the biggest lion ever seen in East Africa. Those lady lions and cubs belong to one of his families or prides. We call him Scarface or Scar because, as you can see, he has many scars on his face. He got the scars while fighting with other male lions. My rangers tell me that Scarface has at least three prides, but I'm not sure."

Stubby said, "With his beautiful long hair, he looks like a king. I'll bet that he is a great fighter."

"You are right," Doc said, "he is a king. He is the strongest lion around. He is the boss. That big rascal is the king and he is beautiful."

Scarface looked proud. The long hair on his head and neck fluttered in the breeze. He took a minute to look around, then he walked toward the zebra

"It is the lion we call Scarface. He is probably the biggest lion ever seen in East Africa." Stubby said, "With his beautiful long hair, he looks like a king. I'll bet that he is a great fighter." "You're right," Doc said, "he is the boss."

kill leftovers.

Scar expected a free meal, so he wasn't happy when there were so few leftovers to eat.

When Scarface got to the zebra leftovers, one lioness was still eating. She jumped up and ran away. But a short distance from the zebra kill she sat down and watched Scarface. A few minutes passed, then the lioness stood up and cautiously moved toward the male lion.

Stubby said, "I think she wants to chew some more on the leftovers. Although she certainly doesn't look hungry."

But Scarface was hungry. He did not want to share any of the food that was left, so he growled and chased the lioness away.

The lioness moved fast as she hurried to get away from Scar. Doc tried to take a picture, but he almost missed. Only the tail end of the mother lion showed on the picture. Doc jokingly said, "This is the end."

Abdi explained to Bobby and Stubby that in a lion family or pride, the strongest male is the boss. If a kill is made, the boss lion, or king, often eats first. If a large animal is killed, the whole pride might eat at the same time. Full grown male simbas are usually bigger and stronger than females, so the lioness doesn't do much arguing.

Doc said, "You should remember that not all lion families behave the same way. Some prides do not eat together. In a pride, the female lions usually do the killing, but the boss lion does most of the eating."

Scarface stood up. He left the kill and walked across the grasslands. When he passed the Rover, Abdi noticed a cut on the lion's side. The warden

looked carefully at Scar's cut side. It did not seem
to be a deep wound, so Abdi did not call the
animal doctor. The lion could easily reach the cut
with his tongue, so it would not need to be
washed. Scarface could keep the injury clean by
licking the cut with his tongue.

Abdi and Doc talked about the wound on Scar's
side. They discussed what might have caused the
cut. Both men agreed that the King lion had been
in a fight. They wondered if the other lion were
dead or badly hurt.

Bobby listened to Abdi and Doc talk. He asked,
"What other lion? I didn't see another lion."

The African smiled. "Scarface," he said, "has
been in a fight with another male lion. Scar won
the fight, and he is still king. When lions fight, the
loser usually is badly hurt or dead. If the loser is
hurt, we want to try to help him get well.

The friends talked briefly. It was decided that
they would try to find the loser. If the simba who
lost the fight were alive, they would try to save his
life.

Abdi and Doc did not believe the loser would be
found. Losers usually move into thick bushes or
down into deep ravines. They stay hidden and wait
to die.

When Abdi saw the sadness on Bobby's face, he
said, "Well, I guess we better get started. We
certainly won't find that lion by sitting here."

Before Abdi started the Rover, Stubby said,
"Would you look at the king? What is that big cat
doing?"

The king lion had walked over to a resting
lioness and sat down. A moment later, he stretched
out his paw and playfully poked her.

The lioness kept looking straight ahead. She did
not want to play. Stubby said, "It is true that lions
are big cats, and cubs sometimes play as if they
were kittens. But big lions do not play very much. I
think Scarface just wanted her attention."

When the friends saw the king cat being playful,
they could not keep from laughing. Their laughter
rolled out of the Rover's open windows and into
the king's ears.

Scar turned his head and stared at the men. Doc
whispered, "Shhh, do not move or say anything.
The king looks very angry. I have never heard of
Scarface coming after anyone in a Land Rover, but
we might be the first ones."

The king lion stood up and growled. All four
men had a good look at his long pointed teeth and
they were all scared.

Scarface was only a few feet away. Bobby
thought he was so close to the king simba that he
could almost reach out and pull his whiskers.

Stubby could feel Bobby shake. Without moving,
he softly whispered to his young son. "Do not be
afraid. It is true that in one leap Scarface could be
on top of our Land Rover, but, even if he broke the
windows, I do not believe that he could get inside.
He is too big to crawl through a window."

Abdi shifted the gears on the Land Rover. Very
slowly, he backed the Land Rover away from the
king lion. All four men breathed easier when the
big simba did not follow them.

Scar followed the moving Rover with his eyes.
When he looked toward the men, it was easy to
see the scars on his face. Scarface is a good name
for the king lion.

As the Rover moved slowly backwards, Stubby

took a picture of two young lady lions as they rested side by side. The eyes of the two lady lions searched across the grasslands. The lions in this pride were hungry. When night came, the adult lions would be hunting. Each hunting lion would move quietly through the tall grass and bushes. The silent killers would probably make a kill before another day was ready to begin.

While backing the Rover, Abdi almost ran over a young lady lion. The female simba snarled in anger at the Land Rover. The African changed gears and carefully drove away.

Warden Abdi said, "Oh, oh! We almost forgot to look for the lion Scarface fought. We better get started."

Abdi began to drive across the grasslands.

Warden Abdi told Bobby and Stubby to watch for buzzards. Buzzards are big rather ugly looking birds. These birds fly in circles high up in the sky. If a dead or badly hurt animal is stretched out on the ground, buzzards usually find it. They eat dead animals.

Abdi explained, "Maybe the buzzards will help us find the lion that fought Scarface. Of course, even buzzards will not be able to see him if the simba has crawled under a bush or under a rock shelf. If he is hidden, watch for Silver-backed jackals. They usually find dead or dying animals that cannot be seen from the sky."

The four friends searched flatlands, hillsides, and bush country. More than once they saw buzzards circling high in the sky, but no big birds came down to eat a dead animal. The men searched throughout the afternoon, but the dead or hurt simba could not be found.

It was late, and the men were ready to return to Abdi's home. The African turned the Rover and headed back.

As they drove along a hillside, they heard a male lion roar. It was an angry sound. This simba was across a small valley.

Doc said, "If that male lion tries to take one of Scarface's prides, there will be another fight. That roaring lion is not friendly. He wants to be the 'new king.' He is actually daring the 'old king' to fight. I'm sure Scar will not run away. He is a proud king."

The bouncing of the Land Rover made loud rattling sounds, but the roar of the lion was louder. Even after the Rover was parked back at Abdi's house, the four friends could still hear the lion roaring.

Abdi told Bobby and Stubby that sounds are important. He said, "When a male lion roars before a fight, it seems to give him more courage. The simba is telling himself that he is the strongest...that he will win."

"Have you noticed," Doc asked, "that only one lion is roaring? Scarface is an older lion. He seems to know that he is big and strong. The king does not need anything to build his courage. Scar has learned many tricks about fighting. He will fight, but the fight will be where and when the king is ready."

Bobby asked, "Do you mean that Scarface doesn't have to be his own cheerleader?"

Doc nodded. He said, "That is just what I mean."

Abdi yawned. "Let's go home," he said. "Scarface almost always fights early in the morning. If we get out of bed early enough, we might be able to see the fight. I think we should go to bed. What do you think, Bobby?"

Bobby agreed. He was very sleepy. The bed would feel good.

Before going to sleep, the two little men and Doc read from God's Word and prayed. The black man smiled as he listened. Abdi was not a Christian. He wondered about this God his friends trusted so much. Someday maybe he would know the one God for all people.

During the night everyone slept peacefully. Stubby even snored, but he did not make much noise. Little people do not snore as loud as big people.

Chapter Five

Early the next morning, Stubby rolled out of bed. He knelt at his bedside for a few minutes while he silently prayed. When prayer time was over, he dressed quietly. As soon as he was dressed, he tiptoed into the kitchen. In the kitchen, he made peanut butter and jelly sandwiches, filled a thermos jug with pop and ice, put frosted rolls in a wrapping, and then tucked a box of potato chips and a jar of pickles into the picnic basket. These things were for lunch.

After preparing a picnic lunch, he started to make breakfast. Stubby liked to cook. For breakfast, he fried bacon and eggs, filled glasses with fresh orange juice, and poured cereal into bowls.

Before the eggs were fried, he awakened Bobby. Bobby was the only late sleeper. Once he was awake, it did not take long for him to get dressed.

While Stubby was making breakfast, Abdi and Doc were also busy. The African warden was outside making a careful check of the Land Rover while Doc checked his camera. The gray-haired man liked to take pictures. He took pictures of people, animals, plants, and places. He believed all of God's creations were beautiful.

After the four friends had eaten breakfast, they carried the picnic basket and camera things to the

Rover. Stubby said, "Oh, oh, I think we have forgotten the binoculars."

Bobby scampered back into the house to get them. During the night Bobby had not slept very much. He had been too excited. However, shortly after the Rover began to roll across the grasslands he became sleepy. He kept blinking his eyes as he looked out the Rover's windows. At times, his head nodded.

Suddenly, Bobby sat up straight! His eyes popped wide open. "Look," he shouted, "look!" His finger pointed toward a hilltop.

Everyone in the Land Rover looked where Bobby pointed. The four men could see a big male lion. It was Scarface. He lay very quietly with a lioness not far from his side.

The hilltop where Scarface rested was beginning to get light, although the sun had not yet risen. Actually, it would be only a few minutes before sunrise would come.

The four friends watched Scarface. Bobby said, "He is big. He is strong. He has long teeth. I know he could easily kill me, but he certainly is a beautiful lion. I wish he were tame like Silver Tip."

Suddenly, another lion roared. The roar was very loud. Bobby and the others in the Rover jumped. Of course, Bobby jumped the highest. Jumping didn't mean he was scared. It was mostly because he was surprised.

When the four men looked out of the front windows of the Rover, they saw a dark-maned simba. The lion held his head above the tall grass and kept looking up the hillside.

The dark-maned lion roared again. Abdi said, "He is daring the king to come down and fight." After his roar, the dark-maned lion carefully watched Scarface.

The king lion didn't even move. He didn't seem to pay any attention to the roaring lion. Although he was being challenged to a fight, Scarface hardly glanced at the challenger.

Stubby whispered, "Bobby, when a lion goes after the king, that lion is called a challenger. This challenger is younger than the king, but he does look to be almost as big. Look at Scarface. He surely does not act scared. He doesn't even seem to be listening to the challenger's roars."

Abdi backed the Land Rover a little further away from the dark-maned lion. They all watched as the challenger slowly crawled up the hillside.

The African told Stubby and Bobby that Scarface had been in many fights. Abdi said, "Scar is a smart old lion. I am not sure that he plans it out, but before almost every fight he seems to make his way to the top of the hill. Whenever another lion challenges him, the challenger has to go uphill. If the dark-maned lion really wants to fight, he has to look up and go up a hill. Climbing a hillside, I think, makes it a little bit harder for the challenger."

Bobby, Stubby, and Doc had their cameras ready. Doc mumbled, "It is still too dark for pictures. I sure hope the fight does not start until after the sun gets out of bed. I have seen simbas fight before, and they usually move very fast. If we are going to get good pictures, we need better light."

Everyone who waited in the Rover knew the lions were going to fight because the challenger had already crawled more than half-way up the hill. It

The lionesses sat quietly in the grass as the young lion growled his challenge to King Scarface. The challenger was trying to build his courage by his loud roaring.

was too late for him to turn around and run.

Bobby whispered, "I hope neither lion gets killed. Both lions are very good looking simbas. It does not seem right that a fight usually means death to one lion. Doc, does the strongest lion always win?"

Doc grinned. "Bobby," he said, "being strong usually helps, but being lucky and being smart are also very important. If we were talking about people, I would say being smart is most important for success in life. Of course, being smart means listening to God's directions."

Now, the challenger was only about twenty meters (22 yards) from Scarface.

Stubby said, "Scarface just moved. He pulled his legs under him. With his legs pulled under, I think he is ready to charge."

What Stubby said was right. Scarface was ready to charge, but he did not go after the dark-maned lion yet.

The dark-maned lion kept growling and roaring as he crept up the hill. Scarface, the king lion calmly rested. He didn't seem to pay any attention to the loudly roaring lion, but, actually, he was watching very carefully every move the challenger made.

"Why," Bobby asked, "doesn't the dark-maned lion charge Scarface?"

Abdi explained, "I think he is waiting for that lioness to move out of the way, but I also think the challenger is afraid. He is waiting for the king to make the first move."

The lioness got to her feet. After a short walk along a track, she sat down. Another lioness came out of the deep grass and stood near the seated lioness.

Doc took a picture. The early morning light gave

his picture a somewhat unusual color.

Almost as if a curtain had opened, the sun's light shone down the hillside. The sun's bright rays shone into the challenger's eyes. The dark-maned lion, for a moment, was blinded. He sat up and blinked his eyes. For a few seconds, the challenger could not see Scarface.

Without even a warning growl, Scarface leaped down the hillside. Pow! Kabam! He struck the dark-maned lion two hard blows on the head and knocked the challenger over backward. The blows were so hard the dark-maned lion was almost knocked out. He was badly hurt. But even badly hurt and punch groggy, he tried to fight back. While laying on his back, the challenger kicked with his back legs as he tried to claw Scarface. The winner and still "king" jumped away.

Scarface stood a short distance from the badly hurt lion and looked at the bleeding challenger. The old lion seemed to know the fight was over. Another victory had been won. This fight had been easy. It had lasted only a few seconds.

After two fights in two days, Scarface acted as if he were tired of fighting. He did not pounce on the injured lion. He did not snarl and growl. He simply turned around and walked down the hillside. As he walked along, Scarface gave a roar like thunder.

Every animal who heard Scarface's roar must have shivered. The roar told them that the king had fought another fight and he had won. Scarface was king of the grasslands.

Abdi drove the Land Rover right alongside the hurt lion. The four friends looked at the deep cut on the simba's head. The cut was from the top of the lion's head all the way to the tip of his nose.

The dark-maned lion could hardly wiggle. His eyes were almost shut. He tried to stand up, but he flopped onto his side. He was still dizzy.

Warden Abdi said, "This lion is lucky to be alive. If he had been able to stand after Scarface struck him, the king would have killed him for sure. He is very badly hurt."

Tears filled Bobby's eyes. He asked, "Will he die? Can't we stop the pain? Can't we help him?"

Abdi, once again, looked at the badly hurt lion. "Yes," he said, "he will die, unless...."

The African pulled a rifle from its case. He carefully aimed the gun at the badly hurt lion. He squeezed the trigger. The gun banged loudly. The dark-maned lion made one small jerking motion, then he lay very still. The lion was stretched out on his side.

Bobby was sad and glad when Abdi shot the lion. At least now the simba would not feel the pain, but he was sad because the lion had to die. Why had Abdi said, "Unless...?"

After shooting the lion, Abdi reached for his radio and called the ranger station. He spoke rapidly in the African language called Swahili. Stubby and Bobby could not understand him.

While Abdi talked to the rangers, Doc opened the Land Rover's door and stepped outside. He started toward the dark-maned lion. The simba lifted its head. Doc really scrambled to get back into the Rover.

"Wow," Doc said, "I thought he was asleep!"

Bobby could hardly believe his eyes. The dark-maned simba had moved. He was not dead. What had happened?

Abdi grinned. "Bobby," he said, "I'm sorry. I

thought you knew about dart guns. When I shot
the lion, I did not kill him, as you can see. I shot
him with my dart gun. Darts are like needles used
by doctors to put people to sleep. My dart gun
puts animals to sleep."

The young boy was very happy. He remembered
that Stubby had told him a little about dart guns.
Stubby was going to shoot Silver Tip with a dart
gun and take him far away if the grizzly did not
like Bobby. It didn't happen because Tip liked
Bobby very much.

Minutes later, a Land Rover, much like Abdi's,
came racing up the hillside and stopped only a few
feet from the badly hurt simba. An animal doctor
and his helper got out of the Rover. Cautiously, the
doctor poked the lion with his toe. He waited, and
then he pushed the lion again with his foot. The
lion was sound asleep. It did not move, even to
wiggle an ear.

Quickly, the animal doctor, a veterinarian,
cleaned the bad cut on the lion's head. Then, with
sharp scissors, he clipped the hair that grew
alongside the cut. When everything was clipped and
clean, he took a needle and thread from his
doctor's bag and sewed the cut. When he had
finished sewing, the cut was almost gone.

The animal doctor spoke to Bobby. "Young
man," he said, "this lion will get well. He will soon
be all right. He might even fight Scarface again.
Maybe someday, this lion will be the king."

Bobby was happy. He gave thanks to Lord Jesus.
Jesus had created the lion, and he had used people
to help keep the simba alive. The tiny boy said,
"Thank You, Jesus."

Chapter Six

Scarface had badly hurt a dark-maned lion in a fight. After the fight, Abdi had the lion sewn up by an animal doctor. Now, the dark-maned lion was going to be all right.

Abdi said, "My rangers will have to feed him for several days, but he will be strong again. If I were that lion, I would stay away from Scarface. The king is still too smart and too strong to be beaten in a fight."

Shortly after the doctor had finished sewing up the badly cut lion, the hurt simba rolled over. The dark-maned lion was beginning to awaken. Bobby, Stubby, Abdi, and Doc climbed into their Rover. The animal doctor quickly picked up his things and jumped into his Land Rover.

Abdi was sure the dark-maned lion would be angry when it awakened, so he made certain his friends were in the Rover.

Stubby studied the hurt lion. He thought the lion's stomach looked empty. The simba was probably hungry. He said, "I do not believe that big cat has had anything to eat. We had better be careful. He is big enough to eat Bobby and me and still not be full." Bobby laughed.

Doc grinned. He said, "One as fat as I am equals more than two of you. I cannot run very fast so it would be easier for the lion to catch me. I'm the one who really should be careful."

Stubby asked, "How long will we stay here? Does the lion still need our help?"

"We," Abdi answered, "will have to be with him for a few hours. He badly needs a rest. He needs time to get his strength back. If we leave him, he could not protect himself. He couldn't even run away. If Scarface or some other male lion finds him, they would finish him for sure. He still needs our help."

The simba opened his eyes. The lion was waking up. He growled and snarled, then he crawled under a thorn bush.

"My stomach," Stubby said, "just growled like an angry lion. I am hungry. Why don't we find a tree to give us shade and eat our lunch?" Bobby, Abdi, and Doc nodded their heads. They all liked Stubby's idea.

The black African started the Rover and drove into the shade of a huge eucalyptus tree. It took less than a minute to pull out the lunch basket. Sandwiches, ice-cold pop, chips, pickles, and rolls were served. Before they began to eat, they thanked God for an exciting morning and the food.

Stubby held up his cup. He said, "Let's drink a toast to the king."

All four friends said, "Long live the king." Of course they were toasting Scarface.

After the last sandwich was eaten, Stubby asked, "Abdi, where do you think Scarface went? It has been several hours. I suggest he could be miles away from here. If the hurt lion is all right, maybe we could try to find him. What do you think?"

Abdi nodded. He reached down and turned the Rover's starter key. The engine started quickly. He drove alongside the dark-maned lion. The big simba was wide awake. The African said, "He will be all right. Let's go find the king. He headed the Land Rover down the hillside.

Warden Abdi drove along a path that went the way Scarface had gone. Several minutes passed as the Rover bounced and bumped over the rocky ground. The little men were having a hard time as they tried to keep from bouncing off the high seat. Stubby and Bobby had to hang on tightly.

When Scarface was found, he had reached a waterhole. Abdi thought that he would drive past the male simba, but when he tried to pass, lions seemed to be everywhere. Every way he turned lions were in his path.

Abdi said, "This is Scarface's pride. My rangers tell me that Scar has more than one pride. I'm not sure, but I know the king travels a lot."

Bobby asked, "What did you say about a pride? I'd like to know more."

This time Stubby answered. "Bobby," he said, "a pride of lions is a family. A pride may have as few as two lionesses, but there might be as many as ten. There are usually several younger lions. Some prides have only one adult male, but there are prides with two or three adult males. Very commonly, when a young male lion becomes an adult, he is driven out of the pride. He roams the grasslands alone until he gets strong enough to fight a pride leader. If he wins, there is a new leader. If he loses, quite commonly he dies."

Scarface continued his walk toward the waterhole. As he strolled along, three young lionesses lifted their heads to greet him. When one of the lionesses sat up, the king flicked his tail. It was a greeting to the lady lions.

A lioness looked down from a ridge. She was very close to the Land Rover. Bobby could easily count her whiskers. Wow! Was he ever glad to be inside the Rover.

Doc said, "It is too bad. Lions are beautiful cats, but poachers are killing many of them. I am afraid the big cats will soon be gone. They are losing the battle for survival. Even our grandchildren may never have a chance to see a big cat in the wild."

Why had Doc said, ". . .soon be gone?" Bobby decided to ask him.

The gray-haired man told Bobby about the big cats. "Lions," he said, "and the other big cats, such as leopards and cheetahs, usually have more than one baby at a time. A group of cat babies is called a litter. Two, three, four, and sometimes more cat babies may be born in the same litter. Just like house kittens, the baby big cats are born with their eyes closed. It takes about ten days for their eyes to open. In the wild country, the young cats face many dangers. Leopards, hyenas, jackals, and several other animals kill unprotected lion cubs. Diseases also kill some of them. The use of babysitters helps. Isn't it strange that killer animals have several young, but the young ones are helpless for several months, and in some cases even for a year or more. Animals that become the food for the big cats, such as gazelles, can run like the dickens only minutes after they are born. Yes, God's Plan is good, but many men are bad. Often, men kill lions just for sport. If people are not careful, God's Plan may be spoiled."

Abdi noticed that part of the lion family was not at the waterhole. He thought the missing lions must be on a hunting trip. The four friends decided to try to find the missing cats.

The tall African drove the Rover through the bush country. He drove across the grasslands for several miles. Finally, he stopped beside a man-made waterhole. There were wildebeests, often called gnus, walking along a pathway near the water. The water's surface was so smooth, it reflected much like a mirror. A picture of the gnus could be seen in the water-mirror.

Bobby looked across the grasslands. He thought that he had seen a lioness duck down in some tall grass. He whispered, "Dad, I think that I saw a lioness. She is hidden in that tall grass."

The lioness did not move. She looked much like a bump on the ground. The big brown cat was very hard to see.

The wildebeests left the waterhole. One of the cow wildebeests walked toward the hidden lioness. Stubby said, "If that gnu goes much further, she will be caught by that big cat."

"I think," Doc whispered, "that wildebeest has already gone too close. If the lioness is hungry, she will catch the gnu for sure."

The gnu stopped. The wildebeest cow seemed to realize that something was wrong. The cow's eyes, ears, and nose searched for danger. Suddenly, the gnu lifted her head high! She whirled around and started to run.

When the wildebeest whirled around, the hidden lioness sprang out of the grass. The female lion moved very fast. She charged across the grasslands. In a few long jumps, the lioness caught the cow gnu. The lady simba threw the wildebeest to the ground. Her long teeth bit deeply into the gnu's

throat. In only a few seconds, the wildebeest was
dead.

Bobby had seen a lioness make a kill before and
this time the young boy did not cry. He was
beginning to really understand God's Plan.

Lions seemed to come from all directions. They
all hurried to the kill. "Holy cow," Doc said, "there
are so many lions, I don't think any stomach will
be filled."

Bobby counted three lady lions and six lions that
were about three-fourths grown. It did not take very
long for the nine lions to eat the wildebeest. The
head, with its horns, the bones, skin, and innards
were not eaten by the lions.

Even before the lions moved away, jackals had
arrived. The silver-backed jackals would help clean
up the left-overs. High in the sky, vultures were
circling. These big birds would join in the clean up.
Finally, the ground itself seemed to be moving as
thousands of ants joined in the clean-up work. In
Kenya, one of nature's clean-up teams is composed
of jackals, vultures, and ants. It takes only about a
day for the bones of a dead animal to be picked
clean.

After the lions had nearly finished eating the
wildebeest, Abdi drove up to the kill. A lioness
turned her head and looked at the Rover. The
African watched her. Slowly, he pulled a rifle from
its case. This was not the dart gun. Warden Abdi
held the rifle ready for action. If the lioness
charged, he would shoot her. The black man had
seen the markings on the lioness. He was almost
sure the lioness had been reported by the Masai
tribe as a killer lion. If she really was a killer of
people, she might even charge the Land Rover.

Abdi mumbled to himself. "I wish I knew. I wish I were sure. If I were sure that she is a killer, I could shoot her now. It might save several lives."

The lions were finished eating. They moved away from the kill. Now the simbas were sleepy. One by one they moved into the shade of a thorn bush, and a few minutes later they were asleep.

The gray-haired man reached out his hand. He touched Abdi's arm. "Rafiki," he said, "what is troubling you? Are you thinking about the killer lioness?"

"Yes," Abdi said, "I am thinking about her. She has already killed three tribesmen. One of those lionesses has several of the markings that the Masai reported. I wish I were sure."

Doc said, "The lioness sleeping under that thorn bush is not the killer. This lioness lives in a pride. She is accepted by the lion family. Killer lions almost always travel alone. Most killer lions have something wrong with them. They have become lame or are getting old. Something is making it difficult for them to make a kill of a wild animal, so they start killing cows and people. The lioness you are worried about killed the wildebeest. She is healthy and fast. No, my friend, I do not believe she is the killer."

"Doc," Bobby said, "you called Abdi 'rafiki.' What does 'rafiki' mean?"

"In Abdi's language," Doc explained, " 'rafiki' means friend. He is my friend."

The sun was low in the western sky. It was time to go back to Abdi's house. When bedtime came, Bobby, Stubby, and Doc read God's Word and said their prayers. The men thanked God for His wonderful Plan. Bobby remembered what Doc had

said...some must die that others might live. The
tiny boy knew that it was also true for people. It
was especially true that Lord Jesus had died for our
sins, so we might live forever. Bobby said, "Thank
you, Jesus."

Chapter Seven

The first rays of sunshine were just beginning to
cover the eastern sky. Morning was almost here.
Doc awakened. The gray-haired man wondered if
he had been dreaming. He could not understand
why, but he was afraid. Tiny beads of water
covered his forehead. He was sure something was
in his room. What was it?

A prayer came to Doc's mind, but he did not say
it out loud. He thought, "Heavenly Father, why are
you keeping me from moving? Why am I breathing
so quietly? Why is it that even my eyes have
stopped their blinking? Lord Jesus, please tell me
what is wrong!"

The gray-haired man listened. He could hear a
clock ticking. It was the big clock that stood in the
hallway. The hallway led from Stubby's to Doc's
room. Each tick of the clock sent a chill down
Doc's back. He wondered why the ticking clock
gave him a feeling of fear. To him, fear was a
strange feeling.

Minutes ticked past as Doc lay perfectly quiet. It
wasn't long before a ray of sunlight shone through
an open window. As the ray came into his room,
the light struck the slender body of an animal.
When he saw the animal, for a moment, Doc did
stop breathing!

From his bed, Doc could see part of the animal's

The swaying head was only a few inches from Doc's bedside. As its head turned, the rising sunlight shone into its eyes. They sparkled like shining beads. It was a deadly spitting cobra!

body. It reached more than twenty inches above
the floor. In the dim early morning light, he
watched the animal's body sway from side to side.
The swaying head was only a few inches from his
bedside. As its head turned to the left and back to
the right, sunlight shone into the animal's eyes.
They sparkled like shining beads. The gray-haired
man had seen this kind of animal. It was a spitting
cobra!

The sun's rays made streaks on the floor. Slowly,
the streaks moved across the floor. From the length
of the streaks, Doc could tell that it was almost six
o'clock. It soon would be time for the clock to
strike. Would the dong, dong of the clock scare the
snake? What would the cobra do if it became
frightened?

The gray-haired man was almost sure the snake
would soon bite him. The cobra was ready to
strike. If the poisonous snake did strike, Doc
believed the poison from such a big cobra could
kill him. From the position of the snake's head, if it
did bite him, its bite would be very near his heart.
A bite near the heart was very bad.

Doc sent another silent prayer to the Heavenly
Father. "Please God," he said, "awaken Abdi. I
need help! If this cobra bites me, the strike would
be very close to my heart. Its poison would
probably kill me. Father God, You are my shepherd.
Please watch over me."

Almost immediately, Doc heard Abdi moving
around in his room. A moment later, he heard
footsteps coming down the hall.

Strangely, Abdi did not go into Doc's room. The
African stopped in the doorway. He stood looking
at his gray-haired friend. Even in the dim morning

light, he saw the beads of sweat on his friend's
forehead. The black man opened his mouth to
speak, but the words did not come out. Two ticks
of the clock later, he saw the big cobra. The
African's eyes became nearly as big as saucers!

Almost silently, Warden Abdi stepped back out
of Doc's doorway. Very quickly, he rushed down
the hallway leading to his room. From a wooden
chest, he took a long bamboo pipe, then he hurried
back to Doc's room. Once again, the tall African
stood in Doc's doorway.

While standing quietly, Abdi blew gently on the
bamboo pipe. A strange sound came from the pipe.
The African was playing music on the pipe. It was
the kind of music played by snake charmers. Abdi
was trying to get the spitting cobra to move away
from Doc's bed, but the snake did not move! It
kept sitting with its head only a few inches from
Doc's side.

The strange snake-charmer music awakened
Stubby. The little man got out of his bed. His tiny
bare feet did not make much noise as he walked
down the hallway.

When he was about to walk past the big clock,
Stubby stopped. He noticed that the clock was
almost ready to dong. The little man glanced at his
wrist watch. According to his wrist watch, the big
hall clock was wrong. He opened the clock's door
and stretched up on his tiptoes as he pushed the
big hand of the clock backward. Now the clock
was set right. It would be three minutes before the
clock struck six times.

Stubby moved quietly down the hallway. He was
listening to the strange sounding music. Where was
the music coming from?

The tiny man walked a little further. That's funny, he thought. Doc isn't a musician, but the strange music is coming from his room.

The door to Doc's room was open. Stubby stopped in the doorway and listened.

Across Doc's room, Abdi was standing in another doorway. He was playing music on a bamboo pipe.

Stubby was sure that somewhere before he had heard the strange music being played by Abdi, but it was a long time ago. The little man tried to remember. Why was Abdi playing strange music on a bamboo pipe? What did the strange sound mean? Why didn't Doc look at his black friend?

Suddenly, Stubby remembered where he had heard the strange sound. It was long ago, but he remembered a snake charmer had played it.

The little man stared into Doc's room. At first, he could not see the snake, but he was sure one had somehow slithered into the gray-haired man's bedroom. Where was the snake? Stubby felt a cold chill run up his back.

Stubby looked across the room. He saw Abdi standing near the head of Doc's bed. The little man was only a few feet from the foot of the bed.

From where Stubby stood, the bright rays of sunlight coming through the open window shone right in his eyes. He could not see, so he squinted his eyes to lessen the brightness. He also shaded his eyes with one hand. Without moving, he searched the room with his eyes. Finally, Stubby saw the cobra.

When Stubby saw the snake, its head was swaying from side to side. It was almost in Doc's bed. The cobra's fangs were ready to strike. The sharp fangs could easily bite holes in Doc's side.

The snake's mouth was only inches from the white skin covering Doc's chest. Stubby had to stop the snake. The fangs must not inject poison into his gray-haired teacher.

The little man did not know what to do, but he was certain that somehow Abdi and he had to keep the cobra from biting! What could he do?

A scatter rug covered part of the floor. Stubby's bare feet were standing on the edge of the small carpet. The cobra was coiled up toward the other end. An idea came into the barefooted man's thoughts. Would it work?

Very slowly, the little man backed off the rug. Slowly and quietly so he would not excite the snake, he bent down. He took a firm hold on the end of the carpet. For a brief time, he prayed silently, then he jerked the rug with all of his strength! The cobra struck at Doc, but the quick jerk on the carpet made it miss him. The gray-haired man jumped from his bed on the side away from the cobra before it could coil and strike again. Abdi and Stubby had saved Doc's life!

Abdi shouted, "Look out, Stubby! The cobra is coming your way!"

The snake was wiggling across the room. It was slithering right toward Stubby. It was moving fast!

Doc yelled, "Run Stubby, run! Don't let it get close to you. If it bites you, it would be very bad."

Stubby started to turn around, but even as he turned the cobra spit red poison at him. The poison hit the side of Stubby's face. It barely missed his eyes. He felt the poison running down his cheek. He lifted his hand to wipe it off.

As he ran down the hall behind Stubby, Doc saw the little man raise his hand to wipe his face. He shouted, "Stubby, don't touch your eyes! Leave the poison alone! I will wash it off for you!"

Stubby heard Doc's warning. He kept his poison-covered hand away from his eyes.

When Doc reached Stubby, he took him into the bathroom. The gray-haired man carefully washed the poison from his little friend's face.

"You are so small," Doc said, "if the poison had entered your eyes, it might have been very bad. Thank God, you are all right!"

Stubby smiled. He knew that God had helped them all!

As Doc finished washing Stubby's face, the two friends heard a loud thumping sound. The sound was coming from Doc's room. They walked back down the hall and looked into the room.

In Doc's room, Abdi held a heavy mop handle in his hands. He had just finished beating the cobra to death with the handle. Before he killed the snake, it had spit at him, but it missed. The African did not miss! He had struck the snake again and again with the handle. Finally, the spitting cobra was dead.

Abdi's shouting, Doc's yelling, and the thumping of the snake with the handle awakened Bobby. The tiny boy came stumbling out of his room. He asked excitedly, "What happened? Dad, are you all right? Where are you?"

Stubby and Doc came out of Doc's room. The little man took his son by the hand. He pointed at the dead cobra. He said, "We had an unwanted visitor."

"Wow!" Bobby said, "It is the biggest snake I have ever seen. Did it bite anyone?"

After Stubby explained what had happened, Bobby went back to his room. A smile was on the boy's tiny face. He was very proud of his Dad. He was sure Stubby and Abdi had saved Doc's life, but he did not forget that God had been present. He began to hum. A moment later, he burst into song. The words were, "Jesus loves me, this I know, for my heart tells me so."

Bobby had changed the words, but he was sure that his words were true.

Chapter Eight

The fight with the spitting cobra made Abdi, Stubby, and Doc even better friends. Each man was sure his friends would risk their lives, if necessary, to help the others. Being willing to face death for a friend is a true mark of friendship.

Stubby said, "Son, I would risk my life for you because you are here and I love you. Think, for a minute, about Jesus. He gave His life for all of us. Even for those who do not like Him. Jesus is the best friend a person could ever have."

Abdi told his ranger friends about the cobra. He told them how something had told him Doc needed help before he was able to see or talk to the gray-haired man. The African was sure that some kind of "spirit" had told him what to do.

After Abdi finished telling his story to the rangers, Doc spoke, "Abdi, it is a Spirit that tells you what to do. It is the living Holy Spirit of God. Someday you will understand."

Abdi had heard the two little men and Doc pray many times. He wondered about this God who was loved by his white friends. It was hard for the African to forget the tribal "spirit gods," but he would listen. Someday, maybe he would become a believer in the one God.

After the dead cobra was taken from Doc's room, the four men dressed. Each man began doing the job he had taken as his part of the work. Stubby's job was to make breakfast. Abdi had to check the Land Rover, while Doc got film, cameras, binoculars, and guns ready. Bobby's job was to help Stubby with breakfast, as well as to help make lunch.

As soon as breakfast was ready, the men sat down to eat. Prayers were said, then they ate quietly. Breakfast was nearly over before Abdi told his friends about his plan to search for cheetahs. The African hoped Bobby and Stubby would soon have the chance to see the spotted cats, but he was worried. The cats with the tear-streaked faces had not been seen for several days. The big cats had disappeared. Where had they gone? Had poachers killed them? There was sadness in Abdi's voice when he spoke to the two little men and Doc. The cheetahs were his favorite wild animals.

Abdi was very much afraid that the cheetah family had been killed. The spotted cats have several enemies. Lions and leopards will kill cheetahs whenever they can. Baboons, wild dogs, and even full grown warthogs sometimes chase and kill the young of these most elegant cats. However, the worst enemy of cheetahs is people. Poachers use trained dogs to chase the cats, snare traps to catch them, guns and poisons to kill them.

Tiny Bobby wondered why anyone would want to kill such beautiful cats. These cats, with the tear-streaked faces, are not harmful or dangerous. He asked, "Doc, why do people kill cheetahs?"

Doc answered, "Bobby, in my opinion, God's most beautiful breathing creations are people. His most magnificent four-legged productions are cheetahs. These cats have feet like a dog, purr like a big kitten, chirp like a bird, can jump high into the lower branches of a tree, although they can't climb, and they can run faster than any other animal. I have never heard a cheetah say 'meow,' but I have heard them cry almost like a child. Cheetahs are very gentle animals."

"Most of the big cats," Stubby said, "hunt at night or early in the morning. Cheetahs have to hunt during the daylight hours. If a cheetah were to hunt at night, it would need headlights much like a car. Can you imagine a cat running seventy miles per hour at night without headlights? I'm sure it would crash into a tree or a big rock. Seventy miles per hour is much faster than a deer runs."

"Zowie," Bobby said, "I can hardly believe that any animal can run that fast. Does it spin its feet and kick up a cloud of dust when it starts running?"

The four friends packed their lunch, cameras, binoculars, thermos jug, and guns and loaded it all into the Land Rover. Minutes later, they were driving across the grasslands. The search for the lost cheetahs had begun.

As the Land Rover rolled along, four pair of eyes searched the hillsides and valleys, but no one saw the spotted cats.

At one time, Abdi stopped the Rover so the little men could watch some buzzards. The ugly looking birds were eating a dead hartebeest. Bobby thought buzzards were mean, angry-looking birds. He did not like the looks of the bald-headed scavengers.

Hours ticked past. Stubby's stomach made a grumbling sound. He looked at his watch. It was nearly twelve o'clock.

Stubby said, "It is almost noon. I'm hungry. How

many think we should eat?" Everyone agreed, so
they pulled out the lunch basket.

The friends were enjoying lunch when Abdi
shouted, "Look down in the valley. Do you see
those tourists? They are getting out of their VW
bus. I think they are going to have a picnic. Do
you see them? They are under that big tree."

Warden Abdi was angry. In a protected area,
called a reserve, tourists are not supposed to get
out of their car or bus. Sometimes special
permission is given, but it takes a written pass from
the Warden. Abdi did not give anyone a pass.

Suddenly, Doc's voice boomed with excitement.
"Look," he said, "look in the valley to your left.
Isn't that a male lion walking toward those tourists?
Abdi, we have to hurry! If we don't get there first,
this may be the last picnic some of those people
ever have."

Abdi shifted the Rover into gear. The Land Rover
spun its wheels and jumped ahead. It raced down
the hillside. The African drove rapidly toward the
tourists. Dust formed a cloud behind the Rover as
its tires dug into the dirt. Stubby and Bobby had to
hold on tightly. They almost bounced off their high
seat.

Stubby prayed, "Lord Jesus, help us get to those
picnickers before the lion does. If that simba gets
there first, some of those people will be killed.
Please help."
"If we hit a hole or a rock," Abdi said, "it will slow
us down. It might even wreck us. In either case,
those tourists will be finished. We have to beat that
lion. Doc, get my gun ready. I might have to go on
foot."

A moment later, Stubby shouted, "I see lion

cubs. They are in the bushes behind the tourists. What will that big male lion do if a cub becomes frightened and cries for help?"

"The big simba," Doc said, "will run like the dickens. If he goes any faster, we will not be able to get there first." He prayed, "Lord, help us get there first. Help us win this race."

The lion began to trot. He held his head high as he tried to see over a hill. From behind the hill the simba could not see the picnickers.

"Although he can't see those people," Abdi said, "I think he smells them. He probably is the baby-sitter for those cubs. Male lions sometimes take care of young cubs. They become baby-sitters while the lioness does the hunting."

The African Warden drove as fast as he dared. The Land Rover roared down the hillside.

Abdi did not toot the horn. He thought the tooting sound might scare the cubs. It might make the young lions call for help. If they cried for help, the male simba would run even faster. Already it was going to be a very close race.

Stubby wondered why the picnickers didn't get back into their VW bus. Those tourists must see us coming. The bus driver surely knows that it is wrong to get out of the bus. Why don't they get into the bus?

The lion reached the top of the hill. From the hilltop, he saw the tourists. With long jumps, he rushed to protect the cubs.

"It is going to be close," Doc said. "If we can cross in front of that angry simba maybe we can save them. Can we make it, Abdi? Can we save them?"

Just before the lion reached the picnickers, the

Land Rover shot across in front of him, then Abdi pressed hard on the brakes. The Rover skidded to a stop.

Doc jumped out of the car. He grabbed a young boy into his arms and hopped into the tour bus.

"Get inside," Abdi shouted. "Get inside, hurry! A lion is after you!"

The tourists scrambled into the bus and slammed the door shut.

As the door clattered shut, the angry male leaped over the front of the Rover. He landed right smack in the middle of the picnic lunch. Pickles, sandwiches, salad, and cake were scattered all over. When the lion lifted his front foot, it was covered with sticky white frosting. The simba's face had frosting on its chin and nose. It was a funny thing to see. It made the tourists laugh, but the four friends were not laughing.

Warden Abdi spoke sharply. "You are very lucky to be alive. You have broken the Reserve's rules. You must leave the National Reserve." The African frowned at the black bus driver. He spoke just one Swahili word. Abdi said, "Quisha!" The strange word means "finished." The driver would not be allowed to enter the Reserve for a long time.

Not many minutes later, Abdi drove alongside the VW bus. Doc slid the side bus door open and climbed into the Rover. The gray-haired man quickly picked up his camera. He was able to get just one picture of the lion washing his face.

Bobby sat staring out the Rover's back window. Excitedly, he whispered, "A lioness is coming. She is right behind us. They must be her cubs. If she has been hunting, I don't think she made a kill. Her stomach looks empty."

When the cubs' mother was near the bushes, three baby lions scrambled out to meet her. One cub tried to get a quick drink of milk. The others crawled under her stomach to get out of the bright sun.

"You are right, Bobby," Doc said. "She didn't make a kill. The whole family, including Dad, is hungry."

While the tourists and four friends sat watching the five lions, Stubby reached out his hands. Bobby, Stubby, Doc, and Abdi made a circle of hands. Stubby prayed. "Thank you, God for helping us save the tourists. Thank you for letting us be present when they needed us. Help the tourists understand that life is wonderful. Keep them from doing foolish things. . .things that may end their lives very quickly. Amen."

The little man wondered why people do so many goofy things. Why do people use bad drugs, drink alcohol, smoke tobacco, and use bad words. These are all things that are done by *losers*. *Winners* enjoy the beauty of life with God. Life with Jesus in one's heart brings great happiness. If people would let Jesus lead them, there would be no need for bad things.

Abdi and his friends watched the lions. The lion family was getting ready to leave. If the African had it right, the pride would look for better shade. The bushes where the lions rested were not thick enough to keep out the hot sun.

Chapter Nine

The lioness, her cubs, and the big male simba rested beneath some bushes. The bushes were not thick enough, so the sun's hot rays shone through them. Lions do not like to be in the hot sun. If you see lions in the daytime, they are almost always resting in the shade of thick bushes, or they are down in a cool ravine. Quite often, simbas sleep almost all the day long. When the silent killers search for food, they hunt during the dark hours of dusk, night, and early morning.

Under the clump of bushes, it was too warm for the lions. The lioness stood up and stretched her muscles, then she called her cubs. The cubs stumbled to her side. Only a couple of minutes later, the lion family walked up the valley. The lioness moved slowly. Even walking slowly, the cubs had a hard time keeping up with the lioness.

After the lions had gone, Abdi gave the tourists permission to pick up and clean up their things. When they had finished gathering their things and cleaning up the mess made by the lion who came to their picnic, Warden Abdi told the tour bus driver to follow him. The African was going to lead the tour group out of the Reserve.

A few minutes later, the VW tour bus played "follow the leader" as it bounced up the hillside behind the Rover.

When the Land Rover reached the top of the hill, the African Warden turned to the left. The VW van continued to roll along behind.

A big smile was on Doc's face when he looked at Abdi. The African saw the smile. He said, "I told them to follow me out of the Reserve. I did not say which gate I would go out. It wasn't the little boy's fault. I think that he should be able to see more of our animals. Who knows, he might grow up and become your country's President. I want him to be my friend, or should I say my "rafiki."

Why did Doc smile? It was because the tall African was heading for a gate that was all the way across the reserve. This way, the little boy in the tour bus could see many of the wild animals.

Bobby, Stubby, and Doc laughed at Abdi, but they all agreed with him. Stubby thought that it would be a wonderful world if all blacks and whites were like Abdi and Doc. The black man and the white man really understood one another. They had a friendship that would last forever.

The Land Rover traveled several miles across the grasslands. It moved slowly through an area where there was no road as it pushed across the tall grass. Thorn bushes could be seen in all directions.

Bobby looked at the sharp needle-like thorns on the bushes. They were more than an inch long and very pointed. He was glad to be sitting on the soft seat of the Rover. It would really hurt if he had to sit on a thorn bush.

As the friends drove along, Doc quickly reached out and touched Abdi's arm. "Rafiki," he said, "I believe I heard something. It is back behind us. Yes, I know you guys will probably think that I am crazy, but please back up. It sounded like the 'chirp' of a cheetah."

Abdi did not laugh. He signaled to the tour bus driver and both cars stopped quickly. This time Abdi signaled to back up. The bus and the Rover backed up slowly. After backing a short distance, Abdi stopped.

Doc stuck his head out the window. He made a strange whistling sound. It was a kind of "peep." It was almost like the peep made by a baby chicken.

Stubby and Bobby could not keep from laughing, but Doc kept chirping.

A whisper came from Abdi's lips. "I see her," he said. "She is up on that high place." The African pointed to a mound. It was not far from the Land Rover. On top of the high place, a beautiful spotted cat sat up in the grass.

Bobby and Stubby stared. This was the first cheetah ever seen by the little men. Bobby remembered what Doc had said. Yes, Bobby thought, cheetahs are the most beautiful four-legged animals. God surely made them special.

When Bobby looked out the back window, he could see the boy in the tour bus jumping up and down. "Dad," he said, "I am sure glad that Abdi chose to go out this way. If we had gone out the nearest gate, we would have missed seeing the cheetahs."

"This spotted cat," Doc said, "has been given a special name. Mr. Ben, an old friend of Abdi's and mine, named the mother cheetah Patience." The spotted lady sat beside a thorn bush.

Bobby said, "What is that in the grass? There are three of them. It's baby cheetahs. Wow! Look at them. They are popping up all over. I think there are five altogether."

Close to their mother, Patience—almost hidden by the long grass—three little cat heads appeared. After a few moments, two more tear-streaked faces were seen. The tiny spotted cubs were very hard to see. They hadn't really been crying. "Tear-streaks" were little marks on the cubs' faces which God designed to help them hide when they were too little to protect themselves.

Close to Patience, almost hidden by the long grass, three little cat heads appeared. After a few moments, two more tear-streaked faces were seen. The tiny spotted cubs were very hard to see.

The spotted lady chirped and her cubs disappeared from sight. She chirped again and the cubs sat up. The mother cheetah sounded almost like Doc.

"I believe," Doc said, "that Patience is teaching her cubs a lesson. She is teaching them to quickly hide when she chirps a danger signal. It's a lesson they had better learn quickly if they hope to stay alive."

"Baby cheetahs," Abdi said, "probably do not give off any odor. Because they do not have an odor, other animals cannot smell them. If they hide and do not move or make any noise, an enemy usually walks right past. From what I have seen, a lion may pass by only a few feet from a hiding cub cheetah without finding it. But it is not long before the baby spotted cats do have an odor. By the time they do have a smell, they can run like the dickens."

After Abdi finished talking, the gray-haired man said, "There are several names for cheetahs. They are often called spotted cats, elegant cats, tear-streaked cats, and hunting cats. Patience has special names. She has been called spotted lady, spotted sphinx, elegant lady, and sometimes golden lady. Although she will not let me touch her, we are friends. She knows that I will not hurt her."

Suddenly, Patience chirped loudly! Five young cubs quickly disappeared into the grass. The spotted lady looked up toward the sky. A big hawk circled above the mother cheetah. The hunting bird screamed. Its screams gave Bobby cold shivers. The "screee, screee, screee, screeeee" sent tingles up and down his back.

"I believe," Stubby said, "that awful screeching is meant to scare the little spotted cats. If a baby cheetah moves, even a little bit, the hawk would probably see it. Hawks have very good eyes and ears. Such a big hawk might be able to carry a cheetah cub, but I'm not sure. However, I do believe that bird has claws or talons sharp enough and long enough to kill a tiny tear-faced cat."

Patience carefully watched the hawk. She seemed ready to jump on the killer bird if it tried to grab one of her cubs.

Abdi was also ready. He had his gun aimed out the window. The African would try to shoot the bird if it tried to catch one of the cubs. With so few cheetahs left in the world, Abdi would try to keep anything from killing even one of the cats with the tear-streaked faces.

Once again, the hawk screamed and screeched, then it dove down into the tall grass. The bird's sharp talons dug deeply into a fur-covered animal. It lifted its squirming catch into the air. The fur-covered animal was sure to die, but it was not a baby cheetah. The hawk had caught a large rat.

Abdi said, "There are many fat rats around. Hawks have to eat to stay alive. We need them to catch and kill rats, but I would not let that killer bird catch a cheetah cub. At least, I would not let it happen if I could stop it."

Patience watched the hawk fly away, then she called her cubs. The cheetah family walked down from the top of the mound. The little spotted cats sat in the tall grass. Four of them looked toward the Land Rover. The cubs were so young that one cub's eyes were not fully open.

"Gee," Bobby whispered, "they are really elegant cats. I wish I could have a cheetah for a pet."

Doc chuckled, "Do you think it would be fun to have a cheetah for a pet? Many times I have wished a cheetah were my pet. I guess you and I think alike. They do make fine house pets, but it is almost impossible, unless you are rich, to keep a cheetah at home. Cheetahs eat fresh meat for breakfast, lunch, and dinner, and meat is very expensive. There are some people with cheetah pets, but these wonderful cats need to be free."

After watching the cheetahs a while longer, Abdi started the Rover. Once again, he drove toward a gate leading out of the Reserve. When they reached the gate, the tour bus had to leave, but the young boy tourist was very happy. He would never forget the big male lion that came to his picnic without being invited, and he would always remember the spotted cats.

The four friends returned to Abdi's house. That night, Bobby thanked God for the cheetahs and for the gray-haired man who could call the spotted cats. During the night, Bobby dreamed about a bird chasing a cat, but the bird was a wren and the cat was a lion. His dream was all mixed up. Even in his sleep, Bobby smiled.

Chapter Ten

The two tiny tourists and Abdi and Doc got out of bed before the sun rose. They dressed quickly, then breakfast was eaten. Not many minutes after breakfast was over, they climbed into the Land Rover.

Once again, Abdi was the driver. He asked, "Where do my tourist friends want to go?"

After receiving an answer, he headed across the Reserve. His friends wanted to go back to the tall grass where Patience was keeping her family.

Bobby asked, "Why does Patience stay in the tall grass? Is she smart enough to understand that it hides her cubs?"

Stubby explained, "Her cubs are very young. She must realize that her babies cannot run very fast. The spotted lady will keep them hidden until they are bigger and much faster runners. Have you noticed that the long hair on a cub's back looks like dead grass? Without question, long grass is a good place for her cubs to hide if an enemy comes after them."

"How could the mother cheetah know that long dead grass is the best place for her cubs? Maybe," Bobby said, "she knows because it is a part of God's Plan."

The sun had barely risen when the cheetahs were found, and Abdi drove right alongside them.

Bobby thought the cheetah cubs were just like kittens. They were very playful. . . and oh so curious. Doc teased them with a shiny metal object and one even ventured a few steps toward the Land Rover, but Mother Patience chirped, and the young cats quickly disappeared into the tall grass.

When he saw the tiny tear-streaked faces of the cheetah cubs, Bobby prayed. He said, "Heavenly Father, thank You for making such beautiful animals."

As Stubby searched the wild country with his binoculars, he noticed that not far from the cheetahs a herd of Grant's gazelles was grazing. As the antelopes ate the grass, Patience kept herself hidden.

After she had watched the herd for several minutes, the mother cheetah quietly crawled on her stomach toward the gazelles. The spotted lady was hungry. She would try to make a kill.

As the spotted lady crawled through the grass, she heard a coughing sound. Instantly, her head turned to the left. The lady cheetah listened with her ears pointed toward the sound. She was no longer interested in the gazelles. Once again, she heard the coughing sound. Patience knew it was the cough made by a lion. Immediately, she turned around and hurried back to her cubs.

When the spotted cat reached the tall grass where her cubs lay hidden, she chirped softly. Scurrying out of the grass, five little cheetahs rushed to their mother's side.

Patience and her cubs moved quickly through the grass. The mother cheetah led her family away from the coughing lion.

The lady cheetah did not run. Even if she had trotted, the cubs would have been left far behind. The lady cheetah walked quite slowly, and she stopped quite often so her stumbling cubs could catch up.

Abdi started the Land Rover. He did not follow the cheetahs through the grass. Instead he drove far

to the left. Now the African was between the lion
and the spotted cats. After driving the Rover
between the two kinds of cats, he turned so his
path would parallel the one taken by the cheetahs.
"Parallel" is like two boys walking down different
sides of the same street or road. If a lion came
after the spotted cats, Abdi would not let it kill a
cheetah if he could help it.

The cheetah family walked and walked until the
cubs became very tired. Finally Patience led them
to a grass-covered mound. There were a few trees
growing near the mound.

Stubby said, "Although those little cubs are
growing fast, I'll bet those are the first trees they
have ever seen. Look at those little rascals."

A moment before, the young cheetahs had
seemed to be so tired that they could barely walk.
But now they were playing like house kittens. One
cat stood on its back legs while it reached up the
trunk of a tree. Another cub sat behind a tree
stump with its front feet resting on the stump.

Bobby smiled. He said, "That little cat looks as if
it were praying. Even its head is bowed a little bit."

The cubs did not keep playing very long before
they curled up and went to sleep.

The young cheetahs slept for nearly two hours.
When they awakened, Doc reached under the front
seat and pulled out a tin can cover. With a screw
driver, he made a hole in the cover.

Bobby asked, "What are you doing, Doc? Maybe
I should be like Bugs Bunny and say 'What's up,
Doc?' "

A big smile was on Doc's face. He said, "You
would never be able to guess, so just wait and
see."

After making a hole in the tin cover, Doc poked
a string through the small opening. He tied the
string to the shiny cover, then he lowered the cover
out the Land Rover's window. The shiny tin cover
twisted and turned as the breeze blew against it.
When sunlight touched the metal cover, it bounced
off and flashed brightly. The five cheetah cubs
could hardly stay away from the flashing cover.

Cheetah cubs are very much like kittens. They're
curious and playful. One cub took a few steps
toward the Rover. It wanted to take a closer look
at the twisting, turning, and flashing cover.

Using the tin cover, Doc teased the cheetah
cubs. He was trying to get them to come to the
Rover. After a few minutes, he pulled the cover
back inside.

The spotted lady arose to a crouched position.
As she arose, the mother cheetah chirped to her
cubs. Very quickly, the young cats disappeared into
the tall grass.

As soon as her cubs were hidden, Patience
trotted toward a hillside. The lady cheetah acted as
if she were going hunting.

Stubby used his binoculars to carefully look at
the hillside. "If she can see an animal on that
hillside," he said, "her eyes are better than my
binoculars. I can't see a living thing."

The spotted lady moved behind a dirt bank.
"Whatever it is," Stubby said, "it is on top of that
bank."

Everyone in the Rover stretched his neck and
tried to see if anything was on the bank.

From his high seat, Stubby stretched the most.
He said, "There is an animal up there! I see it! It's
a Grant's gazelle. Where did that gazelle come

The graceful gazelle spun around. He saw the cheetah coming toward him. Immediately, a cloud of dust arose as the buck rushed to get away.

As soon as the gazelle turned away from the spotted lady, Patience came out from behind the bush and raced at top speed across the grasslands.

from? I must have looked right at it, but I didn't
see it."

"The sun," Abdi said, "is in our lady cheetah's eyes,
and even the breeze is blowing in the wrong
direction. If that gazelle doesn't see her, it will
smell her."

Doc grinned. "Patience," he said, "is a smart cat.
I will bet that she finds a way to get close enough
to try for a kill."

Patience peeked over the bank, then she quickly
ducked her head. The spotted lady began to trot
along while hidden by the dirt bank. She trotted
such a long ways that Bobby almost yelled at her.
He wanted to stop the mother cheetah, because
she was going in a circle around the gazelle.

The young boy heard Doc chuckling, then Doc
said, "Try not to make any noise, but watch that
smart cat. She has gone past the gazelle. Now the
antelope has to face the sun and the breeze helps
the golden cat. Mr. Grant's gazelle cannot see her
or smell her." The gray-haired man chuckled.

Warden Abdi slowly drove the Land Rover
around to the other side of the gazelle. He stopped
where the four friends could see the cheetah and
the gazelle.

Stubby murmured, "There she goes, It won't be
long now."

The gray-haired man smiled, "It won't be long
now...hmm...Isn't that what the monkey said
when he got his tail cut off by the lawn mower?"

Once again, Patience peeked at the gazelle, then
she carefully crawled to the top of the bank. On
the bank's top, she hid behind a bush. The lady
cheetah could see the gazelle through the bush's
branches, but the gazelle couldn't see her.

The buck gazelle lifted his head. With his head held high, his eyes searched the bush country as his nose smelled the breeze. Patience was well hidden so the buck did not see, hear, or smell her.

After a short time had passed, the antelope again lowered his head and nibbled the grass.

Stubby spoke, "Doc, isn't Patience still too far away? I know that she can run like the dickens, but I read that cheetahs couldn't run very far. Is that right?"

"Yes," Doc said, "you are right. Patience can run about seventy miles per hour, and it doesn't take her long to reach top speed, but she has a very small gas tank. Her motor runs out of gas in a short time. Mr. Grant's gazelle can only run a little more than half as fast, but he can run a lot further. If golden lady tried to catch that gazelle right now, she would never get him. It is too far."

A family of crested or crowned cranes landed near the gazelle. The cranes made a lot of noise as they landed. The buck antelope turned around to watch the big birds.

When the gazelle faced the cranes, his back end was toward Patience. The gazelle was facing away from the bush where the mother cheetah was hiding.

As soon as the gazelle turned away from the spotted lady, she came out from behind the bush. She raced at top speed across the grasslands.

The family of cranes saw her coming and jumped into the air and flew away.

When the big birds flew away, the Grant's gazelle spun around. He saw the cheetah coming toward him. Immediately, a cloud of dust arose as the buck antelope rushed to get away. The gazelle

was running for his life. But every second, the
distance between the gazelle and the cheetah
became smaller. Only a few seconds passed, then a
big puff of dust arose from a small ravine.

Stubby said, "I think she caught him. Let's go
have a look."

Abdi drove the Rover to the edge of the ravine
or big ditch. When the four friends looked into the
ravine, they saw Patience standing beside a dead
gazelle. The antelope's head was bent back. The
hungry cheetah had made a kill.

Patience was really puffing. She was almost
completely out of breath. The spotted lady
breathed deeply for a short time, then she came up
out of the ravine. A moment later, the mother
cheetah chirped loudly. Not many seconds passed
before five little tear-streaked faces came running
to their mother's side. As the cubs came to her, the
spotted lady kissed each of the cat faces.

The mother cat took her cubs down into the
ravine. Quickly, the cats drank water from a
puddle. After drinking, the cubs headed toward the
kill. The lady cat called the cubs back. She would
not let them eat.

Stubby said, "Something is wrong. Those cats are
hungry. Why doesn't she let them eat?"

For a brief time Patience stood looking across
the wild country. She listened to all of the sounds
and smelled all the breezes, then the mother
cheetah made her cubs follow her out of the
ravine.

The cubs followed the golden lady until she
stopped in the shade of a thorn bush which was
growing on a hill crest. Patience sat beside the bush
and the cubs lay down in the bush's shade. The

spotted lady looked in every direction, but she did not take the cubs back to the kill.

"Patience," Stubby said, "acts as if she were afraid. Could there be a snake or something down in the ravine?"

"That's it!" Doc excitedly said. "Patience is afraid. The kill is down in a ravine, and she can't see very far in two directions. The spotted lady seems to realize that it is not safe for her cubs to be down in that big ditch. An enemy, such as a lion, could easily sneak up on them. If that happened, it would be almost sure death for some of her family."

"How," Bobby asked, "does she learn all of these things? Did her mother teach her?"

"No," Stubby said, "I don't think many of her tricks and actions could have been taught to her. Patience has a feel. It is a kind of built-in sense for danger. It had to be part of God's Plan from the beginning. It gives the cats with the tear-streaked faces a little better chance to stay alive."

As Stubby talked, Bobby noticed that Doc was nodding his head in full agreement. The two men, Stubby and Doc, were certain of God's presence in everything that happens.

Patience seemed to be staring at the men in the Land Rover.

Doc asked, "Is she asking for help? She sure wants something."

Abdi grinned. He said, "I think that you may be right. Even if she isn't asking for help, I believe she has earned it."

Warden Abdi picked up his radio. The African called the nearest ranger station. He told them to bring a pickup truck to the Lone Tree area. A cheetah needed help.

The pickup truck did not take long to reach the ravine. When it arrived, the African told his rangers to load the gazelle. Abdi helped his men lift the antelope into the truck. The rangers hauled the buck gazelle out of the ravine and put it near the thorn bush where Patience and her family waited.

After the truck had driven away, the mother cheetah pulled the dead gazelle under the thorn bush. It wasn't long before the six cheetahs were eating.

One cub seemed to have a liking for gazelle ears. Bobby said, "That little cat seems to like gazelle ears, but I prefer corn ears."

Stubby, Abdi, and Doc laughed at the young man's "corny" joke.

As soon as the cheetahs had finished eating, Patience chirped. The little cats walked slowly to her side. The spotted lady moved away from the kill. She took her cubs to a mound at least 300 meters (about 328 yards) from the remains of the dead gazelle.

The little cheetahs crawled to the top of the mound and flopped down. With very full stomachs, they soon curled up in the tall grass and went to sleep.

Patience also rested, but she did not go to sleep. The lady cheetah's eyes, ears, and nose were always looking, listening, and smelling, as she guarded against enemies.

Chapter Eleven

When Patience and her cubs had finished eating, the mother cheetah led the five little cats away from the kill. The spotted lady seemed to know that smells from a kill can be carried a long way by the breeze. If a lion or a leopard were to smell the breeze, it could follow the odor with its nose right back to the kill. The cheetah family could not stay near the dead gazelle left-overs.

The elegant lady took her cubs to a mound that was several hundred meters from the left-overs from the kill. From the high place, Patience could see in all directions. The mother cheetah kept watch while her cubs slept.

By the time Patience and her cubs reached the mound, the sun was low in the western sky. At this hour, it was almost time for the four friends to start back to Abdi's house.

It had been a good day for Bobby, but the young boy was tired. Even the wild bush country was peaceful and quiet. The animals who liked the daylight for moving about were getting ready to go to bed, but it was still too early for the night sounds to begin.

In the front seat, Doc leaned back and yawned. He said, "I guess we should start back, it is getting late."

All of a sudden, the gray-haired man sat up

straight. He looked out the window. "Look," he
said, "at Patience. Something is wrong. She doesn't
act like that unless she is afraid."

On the mound, the spotted lady lifted her head,
then she popped to her feet. The lady cheetah
trotted down the mound. She trotted a short
distance back toward the kill and stood for a brief
time with her front feet on a small mound.
Patience tested the breeze with her nose and her
eyes watched while her ears listened for a warning
sign or sound.

A tiny sparrow flew out of the ravine where
Patience had made the kill. Why did the sparrow
fly out of the ravine?

Patience did not wait to see more than the little
bird. The mother cheetah hurried back to the
mound where the cubs slept. She chirped in that
strange peeping way, then she chirped again.

The cubs popped to their feet and moved to her
side. The lady cheetah was frightened. When she
saw the sparrow, she did not need a second sign.
The flight of the tiny bird was enough warning.
Immediately, she began to move further away from
the kill. Patience went at a fast walk as she led her
cubs across the wild country.

As the spotted cat hurried away from the kill,
she did not forget to watch for other signs of
danger. The mother cheetah followed a path that
went through tall grass. If something came after the
spotted cats, the cubs may be able to hide. If the
young cheetahs hid in the grass, Patience would
either choose to fight or try to lead the enemy
away from her family.

The mother cheetah faced the breeze so her
nose could smell any danger that might be in front

of her. Her ears were turned backward as she listened for sounds behind her.

Stubby said, "They have picked a good path to follow. Doc, she seems to be smarter than most animals. Is she really? What do you think?"

Doc nodded his head. "Yes," he said, "she is smarter. Even smarter than most cheetahs."

"Whatever it is that scared Patience," Abdi said, "must still be down in the ravine. Let's drive over there and take a good look."

The African shifted gears and took off for the ravine. When they got to the ravine, Abdi flashed a searchlight into the big ditch. It was not very dark, but the Warden did not wish to miss seeing anything.

"Wow!" Bobby shouted, "Look! It is a big male lion. He seems to be very angry. Patience should be scared."

In the bottom of the ravine, a simba walked along. The big cat was smelling the ground. The lion sniffed the smells left by the rangers, the cheetahs, and the dead gazelle. He stared up the ravine's bank at the Rover and growled in anger, then he jumped out of the ravine.

After leaving the ravine, the lion followed the trail left by Patience and her cubs as she walked from the big ditch to the thorn bush. Under the thorn bush, he found the left-overs from the dead gazelle.

"The left-overs," Abdi said, "from the kill will not last long. That big simba will eat everything and still not have a stuffed stomach."

Although the remains of the kill were under the thorn bush, the lion did not stop to eat. He moved rapidly as he followed the cheetah tracks to the mound where the cats had been sleeping.

When he reached the mound, the simba stood on top of it. He turned and smelled the breeze. Now the male lion could actually smell Patience. He started to run across the grasslands.

"There was food left for that simba," Abdi said. "He isn't just hungry. By his actions, I believe he really hates cheetahs. He must want to kill the spotted lady."

The Land Rover spun its wheels and jumped forward as Abdi pushed on the gas pedal. The Rover shot ahead as Abdi tried to catch up with the lion.

When the Rover got near the simba, the lion roared to show his anger. The roar surprised all four men. It made Stubby, Abdi, and Doc jump. Can you guess what Bobby did? He jumped so high that he seemed to have wings. The boy landed in Stubby's lap.

The male lion rushed along the trail left by the cheetahs. Every leap brought him closer to the cheetah family.

Doc said, "That lion will catch the cheetahs for sure unless we can help. I don't even believe the cubs can hide from him. Although Patience cleaned their faces after they ate the gazelle, those little cats probably have some of the smell from the kill on their feet and bodies. That crazy simba will kill some of the cubs for sure. What can we do Abdi?"

While Abdi was listening to Doc, he had circled to get in front of the lion and now he was heading the Land Rover straight at the big male cat. The African tooted the horn and blinked the headlights on and off. He almost ran right into the lion. This stopped the simba, but only for a very short time, then the big cat continued to follow the cheetahs.

Once again, the Land Rover roared in a circle to get in front of the lion. For the second time, it headed straight at the angry simba. This time, acting on Abdi's orders, Doc held the rifle ready. If the big cat did not stop chasing the spotted cats, the gray-haired man was supposed to shoot to kill.

Abdi said, "We can't dart him because he might catch and kill a cheetah before the drug puts him to sleep, and I do not want to take a chance on one or more of the cubs being killed."

As the rover rumbled toward the lion, the simba snarled and growled. He acted as if he were going to charge the Land Rover, but, finally, he turned around and slowly trotted back to the thorn bush. When he reached the bush, the simba flopped down beside the gazelle left-overs and began to eat.

Stubby said, "Isn't it strange. Patience made the kill. She actually gave that big lion a free dinner and he still wanted to kill her. It is hard to understand."

"Once in awhile," Abdi said, "it seems necessary to help with your God's Plan."

Stubby said, "God must have wanted us to help the cheetahs. He put us here just at the right time. It must have been part of His Plan."

Bobby wondered, when the African grinned, if maybe Abdi was beginning to understand about the Plan."

Patience took her family a long way from the kill. She moved them in a giant circle as they fled from the angry male simba. After a very long walk, the elegant lady found another high mound. The six cats with the tear-streaked faces climbed to the top of the high place and flopped down. The cubs were very tired and soon went to sleep.

Before resting, mother cheetah searched the grasslands with her eyes, ears, and nose as she searched for enemies. By making a giant circle, the wind now blew from the direction where the lion lay eating. The spotted lady could smell the lion although he was a long way from her resting place.

As the night shadows deepened, the cubs slept soundly, but Patience only dozed. Even when she closed her eyes, she never stopped smelling the night breezes and listening to the night sounds.

It was after dark when the Land Rover got back to Abdi's house. The four men did not talk much that evening. It had been a very exciting day and all four men were tired.

Shortly after they had eaten supper, the men got ready for bed. The two little tourists and Doc read God's Word and said their prayers. They did not forget to thank God for a wonderful day. After prayers, Doc returned to his room while Stubby and Bobby stayed in their room. A long hallway separated the two rooms, but with Jesus in their hearts the three men felt bound together with love.

Stubby wondered if he could bring Abdi to God. Of course, the African had a god, but it was not the one true God. His god was not filled with mercy and love like our God.

Chapter Twelve

As the days and weeks passed, the friends saw the cheetahs quite often. Frequently, Doc teased the little cats by using the tin can cover tied to a string.

At first, the cubs were somewhat afraid of the flashing shiny cover, but as the days passed, the young cheetahs became less and less afraid.

One day, a young cub became very brave and came over to the Land Rover. It began to play with the dangling cover by poking it with its front paws. In just a few minutes, all five of the young cats with the tear-streaked faces were playing with the shiny tin cover.

In a soft voice, Doc said, "Bobby, slide forward on your seat. Be very quiet, if you can. Try not to be seen by the cubs."

Bobby slid forward. Now he was very close to Doc. The young boy's heart thumped loudly when the gray-haired man handed him the string. The tiny boy held the string tightly as he teased the cheetah cubs.

It was a busy season for Abdi, so quite often he could not go with his tourist friends. On the days that the Warden could not travel, Doc drove the little men around in his yellow Jeep Wagoneer. The spotted cats became less and less afraid of the two little men and Doc.

Bobby said, "It is too bad that Abdi can't come with us more often. He would like to have the cheetah cubs for his friends, too. I sure wish he didn't have to work so much, but I am glad he chases poachers away."

The young spotted cats liked to play games. They played tag, had boxing matches, wrestled, and played "hide and seek" with one another. It was fun for the three friends to sit and watch the playful cats.

Stubby said, "When we first saw the cubs, they couldn't run fast at all, but now they can outrun almost any animal that might try to catch them, especially if their stomachs are not full. When the cubs eat, they get so full it really slows them down."

One day a cub licked Doc's hand as he held it near the flashing cover. Very gently, the gray-haired man scratched the cheetah's head. The young cheetah really liked being touched and scratched. It began to purr like a kitten.

Several weeks after the little tourists arrived in Kenya, the cheetah family disappeared. Stubby, Doc, Bobby, Abdi, and the rangers searched everywhere, spending many hours trying to find the spotted cats. The men who searched were worried. What had happened to Patience and her cubs?

Because the disappearance was so sudden, the African Warden and his rangers were sure something bad had happened. Abdi believed lions had killed the spotted cats. He thought the cheetahs must have been caught by a pride of lions.

"If Patience is dead," Doc said, "it has to be because of poachers. No lion is fast enough or smart enough to catch and kill the elegant lady."

The gray-haired man did agree with Abdi that some of the cubs could have been killed by a simba pride, but he did not believe any group of lions could catch all five of the spotted cats and their mother.

Stubby agreed with Doc. Of course, he may have agreed just because Doc had been his teacher. Students don't usually argue with their teachers.

Bobby said, "Dad, if you argue with Doc, he might give you a failing mark on your report card."

Stubby laughed. "Nope," he said, "it wouldn't be fair for my teacher to fail me just because we disagreed about something we were studying, so Doc wouldn't do it."

For several days, the friends searched everywhere within the Reserve area for the cheetahs, but the spotted cats were not found.

Bobby's heart was almost broken because he was sure something bad had happened to Patience and her cubs. Each day he became more and more sad.

"Young man," Doc said, "stop being so sad. Patience is not dead. I have watched that spotted lady for more than three years. In my heart, I know that she is all right. The elegant lady, I believe, has had a bad scare. I think that it frightened her so much that she left the Reserve area. At first, Abdi did not agree, but now he does, so tomorrow morning we are going to search an area outside the Reserve. We are going into the lands of the Masai tribes. Little rafiki, you must try to believe me and stop worrying. Don't ask me what it is, but something tells me we will find the lady cheetah."

Bobby listened. "Thanks, Doc," he said. "I will try to believe."

The young lads carried big knives in sheaths. Bobby whispered, "Why do they have such big knives? They sure don't wear clothes like mine. Is that blanket all they have on?" Stubby grinned and said, "They carry the knives to keep them safe from poisonous snakes."

"Is that a buzzard?" Bobby asked, pointing at a tree. Stubby explained,
"Yes, buzzards are the same as vultures...they eat dead animals."

A ray of hope began to shine in the little boy's eyes. Already he was beginning to feel better.

Stubby said, "There is a time to live and a time to die, but only God knows the time. Son, always remember the sparrows."

On the day they were going into Masai lands, the four friends got out of bed before sunrise. As soon as breakfast was finished and cleanup completed, the men carried their things out to the Rover. A few minutes later, Abdi headed the Land Rover toward Masai territory. Masai territory or country is simply a part of Kenya where the Masai tribes live.

Masai country is right alongside the National Reserve, with a small stream trickling along between the Reserve and the tribal lands. On the stream's bank, there is a Masai village. The homes in the village are not very pretty. Village homes are made from tree branches, long, dead weeds, and mud.

It was about seven o'clock in the morning when the four men reached the stream. After finding a flat place in the bank and a shallow spot in the stream, Abdi drove across and entered Masai territory.

The African drove along a path on the bank of the stream toward the Masai village.

Before the tribal village was reached, Stubby pointed to three Masai herdsmen standing beside the trail. They were really boys, but in Kenya, you must remember, the word boy is not good to use.

The young lads carried big knives in sheaths. Bobby whispered, "Why do they have such big knives? They sure don't wear clothes like mine. Is that blanket all they have on?"

Stubby answered, "They carry the big knife, I believe, to keep them safe from poisonous snakes. Is that right, Abdi?"

Abdi nodded. "That is the main reason," he said.

Abdi stopped the Land Rover so he could talk to the young herdsmen. He asked if they had seen the cheetah family. The three lads shook their heads. They had not seen the spotted cats.

One young man pointed to a distant hill. Yesterday, he had seen a flock of buzzards circling in the sky at mid-morning, and not long afterward the big birds had landed. Perhaps they had come down to the left-overs from a cheetah kill.

Abdi thanked the young lads, then he drove toward the hill. He drove quite rapidly because he was excited.

"If a cheetah," he said, "has made a kill, the cats might still be near the carcass. A kill in mid-morning usually is the work of spotted cats or wild dogs."

As the Land Rover went up the hill at which the young herdsmen had pointed, Bobby asked, "Is that a buzzard?" He was pointing his finger toward a big bird that was perched in a tree.

Stubby nodded, then he said, "Buzzards are the same as vultures. They are birds that eat dead animals or carrion."

Abdi drove the Rover close to a flock of buzzards who were sitting on the ground eating the left-overs from a dead hartebeest. The African pulled his rifle from its case, then he stepped out of the Rover and walked to the kill. Warden Abdi carefully studied the dead animal remains, then he made a circle around the carcass and studied the ground. The black man was looking for footprints.

He saw many vulture tracks, then he saw another set of footprints.

Warden Abdi hurried back to the Land Rover. He had a smile on his face when he climbed inside.

"Yes," he said, "it is a cheetah kill and this cheetah does have cubs. Maybe it is Patience and her cubs. We will drive in bigger and bigger circles around that carcass and try to find her."

Abdi drove along the top of a hill as he made a big circle.

Doc said, "If Patience made that kill, she would not go down through that valley. There are too many rocks and bushes in the valley that could make good hiding places for lions and leopards. The spotted lady must be up on this hillside."

At the moment Doc finished speaking, Stubby shouted, "Look! It is the cheetahs!" The man midget pointed to a cheetah face that could be seen as the little cat peeked through the grass.

As the Rover moved toward the cheetahs, the spotted cats began to run away. "Stop!" Doc shouted, "Those tear-streaked cats are afraid. We must not go any closer. It will make them more scared."

Abdi stopped the Land Rover, but the cheetahs moved further away.

Doc said, "More than two years ago, I learned to talk with another bunch of cats. Maybe I can talk to these. The first litter also belonged to our friend Patience. It can't hurt to try. Maybe these cubs will understand me like the others did."

The gray-haired man leaned out the window. He whistled a strange chirping sound. At once, the cheetah cubs stopped moving away.

Doc whistled again. It was a little different tune.

Slowly, the young cats turned around and came back to the parked Rover. They sat so close that the Rover's shadow almost hid them. Very slowly, Doc put his hand out the open window. He kept whistling that strange chirping sound.

One cub stretched its neck and sniffed Doc's hand, then it actually licked his palm. With his fingers, the gray-haired man gently scratched the neck and chin of the cub.

Bobby wished that he could touch the young cheetah, but he was not sure they liked him. He whispered, "Doc, if that cat is afraid, don't you think that it might bite you?"

"No," Doc said, "this little guy will not bite me. He needs a friend. Somehow, the way I chirp to them seems to let the little cats know that I am their friend. Animals are much like people. They need to be loved."

When the cubs came to the Land Rover, there were only three of them. What had happened? Where were the other two cubs?

Bobby sobbed, "Are they dead? Maybe they ran away and became lost."

"They are almost certainly dead," Stubby replied. "If they were alive, they would be here with their mother."

Patience would not come near the Rover. The spotted lady never became that trusting. She knew the men in the Rover would not hurt her, but she also seemed to know that not all people are the same. The mother cheetah was right. It is good that she stays careful. If she became careless, poachers would probably quickly kill her.

Stubby sat watching the spotted lady as she kept looking down into the valley. The lady cheetah

acted as if she wanted to go back through the
valley into the Reserve. But to get back, she would
have to go between all the big rocks and bushes at
the bottom of the valley. She seemed to sense that
it would be easy for lions and leopards to hide
behind them. The way the elegant lady was looking
made Stubby sure Patience was afraid.

The little man said, "Abdi, why don't we drive
down into the valley and check it out. If we circle
around those rocks and bushes, I think we can see
if there is anything that might hurt the cat family."

Abdi drove down into the valley. He drove very
slowly, or poly-poly, as Abdi would say in Swahili.
He even tooted the Rover's horn as he tried to
scare any hidden animal out of its hiding place.
They did not see any animal that might hurt the
spotted cats.

Stubby said, "It seems to be completely safe.
Doc, why don't you call them? Maybe they will
come if you talk to them again."

Doc chirped and the cheetahs came running
down the hillside. A moment later, they raced
through the valley and up the other side. When
they were out of the valley, they stopped running.

The four cheetahs sat near a thorn bush.

Bobby said, "I believe they are saying thanks.
Wow! They almost talk."

Stubby prayed, "Thank you, God. Thanks for
creating the cheetahs and for helping us get them
back into the Reserve." He knew that God watched
over everything. . . even the little sparrows.

Chapter Thirteen

The cheetah family was back in the National Reserve. They had help getting back from Masai country, help that came from the four men. But now only three cubs were still alive. Two of the cats with the tear-streaked faces were apparently dead.

Tears had run down Bobby's cheeks when Stubby told him the missing cubs were almost certainly dead. However, the young man did not feel very ashamed of his tears. Why should he? There were also tears in the eyes of his dad, Abdi, and Doc. Bobby was not the only one who cared about the cheetahs.

Now the Land Rover was parked about 10 meters (about 33 feet) from a thorn bush that grew only a short distance inside the Reserve. Patience sat beside the thorn bush while her cubs rested under it.

The spotted lady sat quietly. She carefully watched a large herd of impalas.

"Wow!" Stubby said, "I count at least ninety of those red antelopes. Isn't that a very big herd?"

"Yes," Abdi said, "I have never seen a bigger herd of impalas in all my years."

Some of the female impalas were recent mothers of kids. In fact, there were baby impalas who were only a few minutes old. These young kids, who had

not yet nursed, were still too weak to run fast.
However, not long after they get a drink of their
mother's milk, baby impalas can run and scamper
pretty fast.

The impala herd leader lifted his head and
looked toward the Ngong Hills.

Bobby said, "Look at his long curved horns. Why
would he be afraid of a cheetah? That herd leader
is a lot bigger and heavier than a full grown
spotted cat. But he won't even fight when a
cheetah tries to make a kill, if what I read is
correct."

"Yes," Stubby said, "it is hard to understand.
Some impalas are almost twice as heavy as our
spotted lady and a male antelope does have long
pointed horns, but he always tries to run away from
a cheetah. Why doesn't he fight when the mother
cheetah catches him? He should be able to win a
fight with a cheetah. He can really battle when he
is fighting another buck impala. No, I do not
understand it either, unless I remember it must be
part of God's Plan."

The mother cheetah crawled along with her
stomach almost touching the ground. She was
moving toward the impala herd. Patience acted as
if she were going to try for an impala kill.

The wind blew from the impalas toward the
spotted lady so the red antelopes would not be
able to smell her as she crawled closer and closer.
The lady cat also hid behind bushes, tall bunches
of grass, big rocks, and, at times, even crawled
along in a narrow ditch as she moved toward the
herd. This made it very hard for the red antelopes
to see her coming.

"Patience," Bobby said, "does many strange

things. At times, she acts almost as if she were a young boy, like me, who is playing 'hide and seek.' There are so many antelopes in that herd at least one of them should see her."

Abdi said, "There are plenty of eyes in a herd that size to look for danger signs, but big herds sometimes get careless. For some unknown reason, at times, they all seem to forget to watch for enemies. Patience will probably catch an impala."

The spotted lady was moving closer as she quietly crawled through the tall grass. All of a sudden, Patience stood up. She came out from behind a bush. The impalas could not help but see her.

With high leaps and long bounds, the impala herd ran away. "Zowie," Stubby said, "some of their leaps must be more than 25 feet long. Isn't it wonderful to watch them sail through the air?"

Patience did not even try to catch one of the rapidly running antelopes. She just trotted toward the place where the red impalas had been grazing.

"Why did she stand up so the impalas could see her? Isn't she hungry?" Bobby asked.

Doc smiled at the young boy. It made him glad to see and hear a youngster who was so anxious to learn. He said, "I believe the mother cheetah is going to teach her cubs a lesson. She will be leaving them someday and there is still much for them to learn."

When the elegant lady reached the tall grass where the impalas had been grazing, she walked back and forth through the long grass.

Almost from beneath her feet, a kid impala scrambled to its feet. Patience had almost stepped on the baby antelope. The newly-born kid had been

trying to hide in the tall grass, but Patience found
it.

The mother cheetah easily caught the impala kid,
but she did not kill it. The spotted lady picked up
the kid and carried it back to her cubs.

"Look," Bobby whispered, "she is letting it go.
Why is she doing that?"

"Bobby," Doc said, "perhaps we should leave.
What Patience is doing will not be fun for you to
watch. You must try to understand that it has to be
done. The mother cheetah is going to teach her
cubs an important lesson. The lesson is on how to
make a kill."

The moment Patience let go of the kid impala, it
scrambled to its feet and tried to run away. But
wherever it ran, the three cubs always caught it. At
times, the spotted cubs and the kid impala seemed
to be playing a friendly game, but the end of this
game would be the death of the young impala.

Often while the cubs were chasing the kid
impala, Patience scolded her youngsters. The
mother cheetah kept insisting that her cubs learn
the lesson. Learning to make a kill is very important
and necessary if the cubs are going to be able to
stay alive.

Bobby was very sad and tears filled his eyes, but
he did not cry. The tiny boy knew that Patience
had to teach the lesson, but it was sure taking a
long time. The little boy was also sure the baby
impala must be hurting very much.

Abdi saw the tears in the boy's eyes and seemed
to understand what Bobby was thinking. He said,
"Young man, look carefully at the kid impala's
eyes. Do you see that they have a whitish or milky
color? It seems that when a baby impala is caught,

almost at once it goes into a condition called 'shock.' It is believed that an animal in shock does not feel much pain...maybe it feels no pain at all. If it were cut with a knife, it probably could not feel it."

Bobby and Stubby looked at the tiny impala's eyes. Its eyes were white like milk colored glass. The young kid was in a state of shock.

Stubby said, "You know, it is absolutely necessary that this lesson be taught to the cubs. So, what made us think God would allow the little kid to suffer? If it were *not* part of a Master Plan, there would be no concern for the feelings of the tiny impala...it would just suffer. But it seems that God doesn't work that way."

Bobby sobbed. He sobbed because one of the cheetahs was biting the tiny antelope's throat. In a few seconds, the lesson ended and the kid impala was dead.

All four men were glad the lesson had ended. It was hard to understand death...even when it was just an impala.

Abdi asked, "If shock is a part of your God's Plan, it sure is wonderful. It saves animals, even people, from a lot of suffering and pain. But Stubby, why do you think your God has anything to do with it?"

Stubby answered, "Rafiki, it is only easy to explain to those who believe in Jesus Christ, but I want you to think about it. Why should there be such a thing as shock to prevent pain unless there is someone who cares? You care...I care...Bobby cares, and Doc cares, but unfortunately *we* can't do anything about it. But when *God* cares, He *can* do something about it.

Bobby smiled. It was good to hear Abdi ask about God's Plan. He wondered if Abdi was changing because his friends cared.

Patience did not catch the impala just to teach a lesson. The cat family was hungry, so they ate the kill. The cheetahs ate almost everything. They gobbled down the innards, meat, skin, and even the small bones. Unless the kill is a large animal, the cheetahs don't leave many left-overs.

All of a sudden, Patience popped up. She looked across the valley toward Masai country, then she chirped softly and all four cats lay flat on the ground.

Stubby shouted, "Do you see them? It's two men! They are walking along the stream's bank."

Warden Abdi grabbed his CB radio. "Calling ranger station number one. Come in, please. Come in, please."

A ranger answered and Warden Abdi told him about the two men. Abdi gave orders. "Get them," he said. "I want to question them. Be careful."

The Warden did not go after the men. He thought there might be some shooting, and he did not want to take a chance on his three friends being hurt, but he watched the two men closely with his binoculars.

A few minutes later, a Land Rover came roaring over a hill. It bounced along the stream's bank as it went after the two men. In the Land Rover, Abdi's rangers were ready for action.

When the men saw the Rover coming, they fired several shots at it, then they started to run. But they soon stopped running and dropped their guns and everything as Abdi's rangers opened fire on them.

The men lifted their hands high into the air. Seconds later, the rangers hopped out of their Rover and handcuffed the men.

Now it was safe for his three friends, so Abdi drove to the stream's bank. He said, "Good work, men. I am proud of you. Ranger Murangu, pick up their guns and the bag they dropped. Let's have a look in the bag."

When Abdi and his rangers had a look in the bag, they found two skins. The skins were cheetahs. Now the friends knew for sure what had happened to the spotted lady's two cubs. Poachers had killed them. The men were poachers.

The poachers told Abdi that an American had hired them to get him two or more cheetah skins. They were being paid almost two years normal wage for each skin.

When night came, the poachers took Abdi, Doc, and Stubby, as well as his rangers to the Hilton hotel in downtown Nairobi. In the hotel, they found the tourist and arrested him.

Bobby had to stay at Abdi's home. He was too young to go with the older men.

When the tourist was arrested, he became frightened. He looked at Stubby and Doc. "You are Americans like me. Will you help me?"

Anger was in Doc's voice when he said, "We are Americans, but we are not like you. We are proud to be Americans, but you are a disgrace to our Country. I'm sure that you know cheetahs are almost all gone. In fact, my grandchildren may never be able to come to Kenya and see a cheetah in the wild country.

Because of people like you, these very beautiful cats are nearly gone. If I could believe that you really felt ashamed and sorry, I would try to help you and so would Stubby. We will pray about it and see you in the morning."

Stubby said, "Mister, you are so wrong. What you have done has already caused much heartache."

When bedtime came, Bobby did not go right to sleep. He kept thinking about the poachers. Although he was sure they would be punished, he hoped they would be all right. He also prayed for the tourist.

Slowly, he drifted off to sleep and into dreamland. In his dreams, he wondered if in God's heaven cheetahs would chase impalas. Of course, the chase would be only in fun. It would be a wonderful race with no death at its end.

Chapter Fourteen

A few days after the poachers were caught killing cheetahs in the National Reserve and the tourist who bought the skins was arrested, Bobby, Stubby, and Doc decided to leave the Nairobi area. They planned a trip into the semi-arid north country of Kenya.

When Doc used the word semi-arid, Bobby asked, "What does semi-arid mean?"

"Semi-arid," Doc said, "means places that have some rain during the year, but it does not rain much so there is not much grass and usually not many trees and shrubs."

Bobby said, "Does that mean that it is probably dry and dusty for most of the year?"

The gray-haired man smiled briefly, then he became very serious. He said, "That might be true for at least part of the year. Where we are going, it is very bad. The rains that usually come seasonally have not come for about two years except in small part. Animals, even people, are dying and on the verge of dying. They need help, but it seems that no one is interested."

On their trip, Bobby, Stubby, and Doc planned to go to Lake Rudolph. At Lake Rudolph, Doc had arranged for the group to go fishing.

"If we are lucky," Doc said, "we might catch a few perch. It might be fun for you. At least, it will be a change."

How could Doc think that it might be fun catching perch? Perch are such little fish. "Gee," Bobby thought, "I think almost anything would be better than to go fishing for perch. In fact, I would much rather have stayed with Abdi. At least I might have been able to see the cheetahs." However, Bobby decided to go. He wanted to be with his dad even more than he wanted to see the spotted cats with the tear-streaks on their faces.

On the trip to Lake Rudolph, Abdi wanted to go but he couldn't. He was too busy trying to catch poachers. It was very hard for Abdi and his rangers to protect the wild animals.

The three friends packed what was needed into Doc's yellow Jeep Wagoneer. The Wagoneer had built-in beds, a stove, cooking pans, a gas lantern, an ice chest, thermos jug, and other things that made camping easy. In fact, the Jeep was almost like a small hotel.

When the Jeep left Abdi's house, all three men sat in the front seat. Stubby and Doc had fixed part of the front seat for the little men making part of the seat higher. It was comfortable and easy for them to see out.

At first, the Wagoneer rolled along the highway at a fast pace, but after traveling for several hours the speed became much slower. The road had changed. It had become more narrow, crooked, rocky, and very dusty. When the Jeep moved along—even slowly—clouds of dust flew up from beneath its wheels.

Stubby looked out the Jeep's windows. He said, "It does not look as if anything could live in this place. I can't see a patch of green anywhere. It is almost like a desert. It is easy to understand why animals and even people are dying. This is terrible."

The entire countryside was brown. Dust covered the twigs of the few bushes growing by the roadside. The ground was covered with rocks and stones. Even driving very slowly, dust came into the Jeep. It stuck to the corners of the three men's eyes and to their lips and noses.

Doc said, "Reach into that box. There are masks to cover our noses and mouths. We are lucky. We do not live here or have to stay here. It must be awful for anything to try to live here."

Before they could cover their noses and mouths with the masks, Stubby pointed to a group of tribal people. They were camped along the roadside.

Doc stopped the Jeep.

Bobby asked, "Is it safe to get out? Even the women and children look hungry, thirsty, and sad. Isn't there some way we could help them?"

"Look around." Doc said, "If you see any young men, we must be very careful."

Bobby looked around at one side of the roadway, while Stubby looked at the other side. All they could see were women, children, and a few old men. None of them carried spears.

"I think," Doc said, "that it is safe. The young men and the cattle must be further down the roadway. When you walk among the rocks, be careful of snakes. There are puff adders in this area and they are very poisonous snakes.

Bobby, Stubby, and Doc stepped out of the Jeep. They walked to a tribal house. It was really a very small hut that was made with branches and skins.

"I am a midget," Bobby said, "but I would have a hard time getting into that kind of a house. Even

little people like Dad and me would have to duck
our heads to get inside."

The tribal peoples were much taller than Bobby.
If they had to go inside, it was necessary for them
to crawl on their hands and knees.

A young African woman pointed to the two little
men. She said, "Totos?"

Doc shook his head. He pointed his finger at
Stubby and Bobby, then he said, "Bwanas."

The young woman had called the midgets
children. Doc had called them men. There was a
puzzled look on the black lady's face.

Near the tribal camp, donkeys, camels, and goats
searched for something to eat. All of the animals
seemed to be on the brink of starvation. Many
were almost dead.

Doc explained, "As I told you before, it has been
very bad for these people and their animals. For
almost two years, there has been very little or no
rain. This area is always quite dry, but it is much
worse now. As you can see, already quite a few of
the animals have died. Even some of the tribal
people are dead, especially the old people. In times
like these, old people often just sit down and
refuse to eat or drink. Of course, they die, but it
leaves a little more food and water for the younger
members of the tribe. If conditions get worse, even
tiny babies may be left under a bush to die.

An African woman walked across the rocky
ground carrying a calf. The calf was so weak that it
could not walk.

Bobby asked, "Why don't they let the weak
animals die, or kill them? If they did, it would
leave more food and water for the stronger
animals. Wouldn't that be a good idea?"

Stubby said, "Your idea might be all right for *animals,* but of course it could *never* apply to *people,* because if it did, what would happen to two weak little midgets? What would happen to old people? Where would it stop? What about the lame or the deaf or the blind? Should we also let the sick people die? Who would do the choosing of the people with the greatest value? Remember, one of the world's greatest musicians was a blind man."

Bobby wondered if people would ever choose to kill old folks and those that are weak. He thought that if man gives up his belief in God, such killing could possibly happen. But then he smiled. He was sure God would always be ready to help. But what if people didn't ask for His help? He thought love would die. The little boy was sure glad that Jesus loves everyone, even tiny midgets.

The African tribe was getting ready to move. It was a nomadic tribe. Nomadic means to move from one place to another. This tribe had to move from place to place because it was their only chance to keep alive. There was never enough grass and water for their animals, so they had to keep searching.

When the tribe moved, usually the young men drove the cattle and left first. After they had gone, the women, children, and a few old men folded up the small huts and tied them on the backs of donkeys and camels. As soon as everything was loaded, the women, children, and old men followed along behind the young men and the cattle herds.

For a while, Bobby, Stubby, and Doc drove along behind the tribal people. About noon, the nomadic tribe came to a bore hole. A bore hole is a place to get water. It is a deep hole that has been dug or drilled into the ground. At the bore hole, the tribal peoples and their animals were getting a drink of water. The hole was too deep for the animals to go down to the water, so African men and women were busy carrying water up out of the hole.

Young girls were also working hard. They were filling large jugs. The water containers had been woven from grasses. The containers were tied on the backs of camels. The camels had to get down on their stomachs so the girls could reach high enough to fill the jugs.

Bobby asked, "What if the bore hole dries up and there is no more water?"

Stubby answered, "Thousands of animals and many people would die. It would be terrible. Let's hope that it does not happen."

The tiny boy looked at his thermos bottle. He realized that such a little bit of water could not help. He wondered why people tried to live in such an awful place.

Stubby told him, "These people are free and freedom is a wonderful thing. These tribes are willing to suffer to keep their freedom, but it isn't only freedom. These peoples have no job training skills. If they were to move to the city, there would be nothing for them to do. Education is a very important thing. You cannot earn unless you are willing and able to learn."

Doc said, "If we Americans ever lose our will to fight to keep our freedom, we will have lost everything. Without freedom, life is without meaning. Without freedom, we couldn't even worship our God openly. I think God wants us to be free."

The gray-haired man shifted gears and stepped

harder on the gas. Although he did not drive fast, the yellow Jeep soon left the tribal people behind.

The Jeep moved along a very dry, dusty road. Soon it came to a small African village. This was the next stopping place for the three friends. At the village, they were going to meet an African college student. The student, Cornelius, was a friend of Doc's. He was going with the three men almost all of the way to Lake Rudolph.

As the Wagoneer rolled along the rough dirt road toward the Lake, Cornelius sat up front with Doc. Bobby and Stubby stretched out on the bed in the back part of the Jeep. "Boy," Bobby said, "this is real soft and comfortable. I would call it solid comfort!"

Suddenly, Doc pushed hard on the brakes. The Wagoneer skidded to a stop.

Bobby yelled, "What's the trouble, Doc? What do you see? Is everything all right?"

Three African men were standing on the road. The black men had leaped out of the ditch beside the road. In their hands, they held long spears and big sharp knives.

Cornelius whispered, "They are warriors and for some reason they are angry. Do not get out of the Jeep until I have talked to them"

Bobby was frightened. He rolled over closer to Stubby.

Slowly, Cornelius got out of the Jeep. He began talking to the warriors. "Jambo, rafiki," he said. But even as he talked to them, the warriors kept moving closer to the Jeep. The tribesmen held their spears with the points aimed at the Wagoneer. Were the men going to stick the sharp spears into the front of the Jeep?

Very softly, Doc said, "Stubby, hand me one of your thermos bottles. Hurry! These warriors are really angry about something. Maybe a cold drink will help cool them off."

The gray-haired man took the thermos from Stubby. Quickly, he poured ice-water into a paper cup, then he held the full cup out the window. One of the warriors looked into the cup. He took the cup from Doc's hand and drank the cold water. Doc gave water to all three of the warriors, but their anger did not end.

Cornelius said, "They are angry because not more than an hour ago some white people in a tour bus passed them. The people threw things and laughed at them. The tourists also called them boys."

Stubby said, "Give them each one of these. Perhaps, you should give them at least two." He handed Doc a box of sugar lumps.

Doc handed two lumps of sugar to each warrior, but the tribesmen did not put the sugar lumps in their mouths. Instead, the warriors looked even more angry as they watched Stubby and Doc.

Stubby said, "Maybe if we both eat a lump, they will get the idea. Let's put one in our mouths. I'm ready if you are. Cornelius, you can tell them it is good."

The tribesmen watched Stubby and Doc suck on the sugar lumps. Finally they put the lumps into their mouths. As the sweet taste filled their mouths, a big smile slowly covered their black faces. The African tribesmen were no longer angry. They smiled at the three white men and Cornelius.

Cornelius said, "You know one reason why the tribesmen were angry, but they have another reason. These men have just caught and killed some cattle thieves. It is foolish, but it is their way of life. African tribes often steal from one another and when they get caught, someone usually dies. It is kind of a game with them. Of course, it is wrong, because people die, but to them it is almost like a contest."

After asking Cornelius a few questions, Doc thought that it would be safe to get out of the Jeep. He stepped out onto the dry, dusty, and hot land. A moment later, Doc had his arm around a warrior while Stubby took a picture.

Bobby whispered, "Look at the way they fix their hair in long stringy braids. Wow! Do you see those earrings? I'll bet big bone earrings like those really hurt their ears."

After the warriors had gone, Doc drove on down the road until he came to Lake Rudolph. When they reached the Lake, they camped right on the shore. After a swim, they ate and soon went to bed.

Before Cornelius left, they all read God's Word and prayed together. They prayed for God to send rain.

As the three men tried to sleep, the sound of drums and chanting rumbled along the lake shore. Many Africans were doing a rain dance, as they tried to make it rain. If they believed in the real God instead of believing in "witch doctors," the real God would probably help them . . . if it was a part of His Plan.

Tears were in Bobby's eyes. Maybe, someday, he could teach these tribal people about the real God. For a moment, he even wished that he were a big people. It would be hard for a midget to be a mission worker, but maybe people would listen to a little man.

Chapter Fifteen

The next morning the little men got up early and dressed, then they went to the lakeshore. As the two tourists looked across Lake Rudolph, sunrise painted a beautiful picture in the sky and on the water. The lake was colored by the golden sun's rays and Bobby tried to take pictures of the colorful sky and water.

Stubby said, "God paints the most beautiful pictures. He is the best Artist of all. I do not believe that it is possible for any artist or photographer to take a picture as wonderful as those He paints."

After returning from the lake, the little men joined Doc for breakfast. A few minutes later, they hurried to the boat dock and rented a boat and fishing poles and bought some fish bait. When the boatman said, "All aboard!" the three men were ready so they hopped into the motor boat.

The African piloting the boat slowly pulled away from the dock. When all was clear, the motor boat roared into action as it pushed its way out into deep water.

Bobby had never seen such a big lake. He couldn't even see where the lake ended. He said, "Dad, are you sure that this is a lake? I think it is an ocean. Where does it end?"

"Lake Rudolph," Stubby said, "is more than 150

miles long, but it is skinny. It is a big lake, but oceans are much bigger."

When the boat reached deep water, the boatman slowed it down. Bobby, Stubby, and Doc put their fishing lines into the lake. The lines were pulled along behind the boat. This kind of fishing is called "trolling."

Bobby asked, "If we are going to catch perch, which are little fish, why are we using fishing lines that are so strong? It seems as if my fishline is strong enough to hold a whale."

Not long after the three tourists started trolling, a fish grabbed the bait and hook on Bobby's line.

Bobby yelled, "I've got one! I've got one! Somebody help me. I can't hold it."

Although Bobby pulled hard on his fishline, the tiny fisherman could not pull the fish into the boat, so the boatman grabbed Bobby's fishing pole. He helped the little fisherman land the fish.

"Wow!" Bobby said. "Is that a perch? Perch are supposed to be little fish. How much does it weigh? It sure is a whopper."

The fish actually weighed 33 pounds. It was almost as long as Bobby is tall.

After Bobby caught the perch, for some unknown reason, there were no more fish caught. More than an hour passed as the boat moved slowly across the small waves which gently rocked the boat. The rocking motion was almost like the rocking of a cradle. It made the men sleepy. First Bobby and then Doc fell asleep.

Stubby also became sleepy, but before the little fisherman dozed, he tied his fishing line around his leg. The knot he tied would come untied when a fish pulled on the line, but the little man was sure it would wake him up.

After tying the line around his leg, Stubby went to sleep. In his sleep he crossed and uncrossed his legs, this caused the line to become tangled.

Before Stubby's snoring had really begun, a big fish grabbed the hook on his fishline. The tangled line became very tight on his leg as the fish jerked him off his seat and began to pull him toward an open place in the boat's deck rail.

"Help! Help! Help!" Stubby shouted, as he slid across the deck.

When Stubby shouted, Bobby's eyes popped open wide while Doc quickly jumped to his feet.

Bobby and Doc saw Stubby sliding across the deck on the seat of his pants. The fish was pulling the little man toward the lake. At once, Doc flopped down on top of the little man. He held the little man tightly. But the little fisherman still slid along the deck toward the water, although Doc almost stopped his sliding motion. If Stubby were pulled into the lake, the gray-haired man was sure his little friend would be drowned.

Bobby looked at the strong fishline that was tangled around Stubby's leg. The fish was pulling so hard that the line was beginning to cut his Dad's leg. With his fingers, the young boy tried to loosen the line, but he couldn't get it loose.

The boatman grabbed a big knife and hurried to cut the line, but he slipped on the wet deck and fell. The knife was knocked from his hand. It bounced along the deck and plopped overboard into the lake.

Things were happening so fast the little boy did not know what to do, so Bobby prayed. He cried with his heart to Lord Jesus. All he said was, "Jesus,

Jesus, Jesus."

Doc put his body between the gap in the boat's rail and Stubby. The gray-haired man was lying flat on his stomach. Stubby was pressed tightly against Doc's side, but he was no longer sliding toward the water. Doc said, "Bobby, we've got him stopped, but now we have to get him loose."

Water splashed against Doc's left hand as it hung down over the side of the boat. Without being able to see what he was doing, he ran his fingers along the boat's edge until they touched the fishline. He tried to pull the line so it would be loose on Stubby's leg, but he could not pull it with one hand. The wet line was too slippery and it cut into his fingers until they bled.

As he lay on his stomach, he felt his own body slide just a wee bit. He thought the fish must be pulling extra hard so Doc stiffened his muscles and refused to be moved.

Being very careful to keep his body between Stubby and the edge of the boat, the gray-haired man squirmed onto his side. He grabbed a rag that the boatman threw to him. Quickly, he wrapped the rag around his fingers, then he spoke to Stubby and Bobby.

When Doc turned his head, he saw Stubby's face. It was white with pain. The little man seemed about ready to faint.

Doc said, "Hang in there. God is with us. When I pull on the fishline, you must get yourself untangled. Are you ready? I'll nudge you with my shoulder when I'm all set."

A flush of color came into Stubby's cheeks and strength seemed to flow into his tiny legs and arms. The little man even smiled as he said, "Yes,

I am ready."

The gray-haired man's eyes closed and his lips moved in a silent prayer. He said, "God, please give me strength."

While holding the fishline in both hands, he nudged Stubby, then he pulled as hard as he could as he tried to slow the fish and slacken the line that had been pulled so tightly around Stubby's leg.

Although his face became wrinkled with pain as the fishline squeezed his fingers tightly together, Doc slowed the swimming fish and got some slack in the line.

Stubby felt the line loosen around his leg. Quickly, he untangled it. The tiny man was free. He rolled away from Doc's side and staggered to his feet.

Doc let go of the fishline and rolled over until he lay flat on his back.

Bobby jumped up and down. He turned his eyes toward the blue sky then he shouted, "Thank you, Jesus."

While Doc was still lying on the deck, Stubby and Bobby knelt down beside him. The gray-haired man reached for the little fishermen with his bleeding hands. Stubby took one hand then Bobby held the other. With their hands joined together, they gave thanks to their Lord.

The African boatman shouted, "The fish is still on the line. Let's try to get it in the boat."

The boatman grabbed Stubby's fishing pole. He struggled with the fish, but, finally, he was able to get it into the boat.

When Bobby saw the fish Stubby had caught, he said, "The fish I caught must be a midget." Everyone laughed.

The fish Stubby caught was a perch, but it was a Nile perch. Nile perch get to be big fish. It is no fish story when I tell you that Stubby's fish weighed 172 pounds (or almost 80 kilograms).

Stubby grinned. He said, "That is the first fish that ever caught me before I caught it."

The cuts on Stubby's legs were not bad and Doc's fingers were not badly hurt either, but the cuts were cleaned and bandaged to keep them clean.

When Stubby thought about the blood on Doc's hands, it made him think about Jesus Christ. The gray-haired man had given a little of his blood to save the little fisherman's life, but Lord Jesus had gone to the cross and given all of His Pure and Perfect blood to save us all.

After they read God's Word, the three men prayed together again when bedtime came. After prayers, Bobby did not go right to sleep. He thought about Jonah and the whale.

"Dad," he asked, "I think that big Nile perch could almost swallow a little guy like me, so it would be easy for a whale to swallow Jonah. Whales are huge compared to a perch. Don't you think so, too?"

Stubby reached across the space between them. He touched his son's hand. "God," he said, "can do anything. He can make anything happen that he wants. There are no problems. Even science has demonstrated that a whale could do just as the Bible says about Jonah. Remember there is nothing God cannot fix."

Chapter Sixteen

The morning after Stubby caught the Nile perch, the two little fishermen arose early. They wanted to watch the sunrise as it cast its light on the waters of Lake Rudolph. Yesterday's sunrise had been so beautiful that they hoped to see another much like it.

While standing on the shore of the lake, the tiny father and son gave thanks to their Creator. In Bobby's prayer, he said, "Heavenly Father, thanks for giving me life and an appreciation for nature's beautiful pictures. In everything that I do, make me always remember that I belong to You."

When they returned to camp, Doc had the Wagoneer all packed. It was ready to roll. A moment later, the little men and Doc were all set to leave the shores of Lake Rudolph.

Bobby asked, "Where did you say we were going? Was it into another country?" Doc answered, "Yes, I had planned to cross the border into another East African country, but perhaps we should not go. Across the border many people have been killed, while thousands of families have been forced to flee from the country. The country's leader is a cruel and heartless man. His government has caused much trouble."

Stubby and Bobby talked to one another, then one little man said, "We are God's children. God will be with us all the way. Doc, if you are willing to go, we would like to see with our own eyes just what is really happening."

The gray-haired man said, "Border patrol station here we come."

On the way to the station, the roadway is crossed by a painted line. This line marks the location of the earth's equator. The equator is like a belt that reaches around the earth's stomach. It divides the earth into two halves.

When they reached the equator, Doc stopped the Jeep. He climbed out and stood beside a sign that marked the equator. Stubby and Bobby took pictures of him.

The stop at the equator was for only a few minutes, then the Jeep was headed down the highway toward the border patrol station that separated Kenya from its neighboring country.

When the Wagoneer reached the station, the Kenyan border patrol guards smiled at the three Americans. A moment later, the Corporal in charge came out of his office. When Doc saw the young officer, he said, "Jambo rafiki. Do you remember me?"

The young African ran to the gray-haired man. They clasped hands firmly as the black man bowed and gave a salute of honor. Doc had been the Corporal's teacher several years back into the past. Bobby whispered, "Dad, I hope that I am color-blind like Doc. He loves people no matter if they are black, brown, or white."

After a brief visit, the Kenyans waved goodbye and the Jeep rolled ahead. This time it moved very slowly, as it moved toward the neighboring country's border. In this station, the border guards were not very friendly. The guards checked everything that the Wagoneer carried. But the patrolmen did not take anything. Finally, they let the three Americans drive across the border and enter their country.

In this country, Doc drove very slowly. He was even more careful not to break any laws. In a strange country, it can be very bad to be arrested. He said, "We must be very careful. We will go slowly or 'poly poly,' so there should be no trouble."

Because Doc drove poly poly, it took quite a long time for the travelers to reach the outskirts of the country's Capital City.

On the outskirts or edge of the Capital City, the army had set up a roadblock. Big boards with nails sticking out of them had been placed across the road. If a car were to try driving over the boards, its tires would be poked full of holes. Every car coming out of the City had to stop.

At the roadblock, the soldiers made all of the persons who were trying to leave the City get out of their cars. Every bag, box, suitcase, and package was taken from the cars and emptied on the ground.

Soldiers were everywhere. When a brown-skinned man began to weep, a soldier lifted his gun and shot him. The man fell to the ground. Now, he lay dead beside the road.

The dead man's family stood by the road. The women and young children were crying, but the young men did not cry.

Doc whispered, "If men cry or act afraid, they are thought to be cowards. Even out in the native villages cowards are commonly killed. We must pray that God will give us strength so our fear does not show if they come after us."

After killing the brown-skinned man, the guards took his money, rings, and watch, then they lined up his family members. Rings, beads, purses, watches, bracelets, earrings, and extra clothing were taken from them. They also took the family's car, then the family was made to walk along the road leading out of the country. It would be days before the walkers reached Kenya.

Again Doc whispered. He said, "Here they come. Please God help us." With his heart, he had spoken to his Lord. Stubby breathed a deep sigh, then he said, "Yes, Jesus, we need you. Amen."

Just before the soldiers reached the Jeep, Doc opened the door and started to get out, but he was pushed back inside and the door was slammed shut.

With a crisp tone of voice, Doc spoke in Swahili. He said, "Soldiers, I am a friend of some of your leaders. Check my papers carefully. They contain a note from your President. It permits me to travel in your country. Do not get in our way or I will report you to your superiors."

When things did not happen quickly, Doc shouted, "Where is your commanding officer? I want to speak to him at once!"

The soldiers seemed surprised and confused. They smiled while backing away from the Jeep. One soldier called to his commanding officer. The officer hurried over to the Jeep.

When he reached the Wagoneer, he stopped. In very clear English he asked, "Are you Americans? Do you have a permit?" Stubby and Doc nodded to both of his questions.

Doc talked to the commanding officer. He used the African's language. By using the officer's language, the gray-haired man was showing respect for him.

The officer smiled, then he gave orders. Quickly, the boards with the long nails were moved to one side so the Jeep could roll on down the road.

The gray-haired man thanked the officer, then he drove into the Capital City.

Bobby said, "Gee, I was surely scared. There were rifles, machine guns, long knives, hand grenades, and pistols all over the place. Those soldiers must really hate the brown-skinned people. It sure is bad when a man is shot." Bobby cried.

As Bobby cried, Doc spoke to him in a soft tone of voice. He said, "Trying to act brave might be a foolish thing to do in some parts of the world. However, I understand these people. If we had not acted brave, they probably would have killed us— even with the permit from their President. They respect brave people. You were very brave. If a boy can act brave, even though he is scared, he must be brave. Remember, it might be very foolish to act the way we did. You must know and understand the people."

When Doc had finished speaking, Stubby said, "Bobby, I was pretending. Yes, I was shaking in my shoes, but I trusted Doc. Remember, he was my teacher. I want you to always remember what he tells you. But right now, I think we should give thanks to God for watching over us. We must also pray that all people will learn to love one another. If we could all be Christian brothers, most of the world's problems would go away. As Christians, people would not let skin color make a difference.

Yes, we would love instead of showing hate."
Silently Bobby, Stubby, and Doc prayed.

The three Americans did not stop in the big,
bustling city. They followed a highway that led
them through the city and out the other side as
they headed toward the rushing waters of the Nile
River. If everything went all right, that night they
would make camp on the bank of that great river.

Hours later, they stopped on the Nile's bank.
Quickly, Bobby hopped out of the Jeep. He ran to
the water's edge. Suddenly, he stopped and stared
at the soft ground near the river's shore.

In the soft ground, there were many footprints.
The footprints were sunk deeply into the soft
ground. They formed pathways that led through the
thick grass. What had made the footprints and
pathways? Bobby ran to ask Stubby.

When Bobby asked his first question, Doc
answered, "Hippopotamuses," he said, "come out
of the river during the night. The big 'river horses,'
as they are sometimes called, eat the grasses and
bushes that grow on the bank near the river's edge.
Those paths are made by the hippos. When we
camp tonight, we must be careful not to park too
near one of those river horse pathways. Hippos are
big strong animals. They can be very dangerous."

For his second question, Bobby asked, "How did
they get named 'river horses'?"

This time Stubby answered. He said, "the
meaning of the word 'hippopotamus' is 'river horse.'
But people do not ride on river horses. However,
hippos actually do trot along on the bottom of
rivers and ponds where they swim. Yes, they really
do have pathways on the bottom of the Nile
River."

During the late afternoon and early evening hours, Bobby, Stubby, and Doc saw many hippos, crocodiles, and many kinds of birds, but all the big animals stayed away from the camp so it was a peaceful time of day.

After the three men had gone to bed, an almost full moon lighted the campsite. In the middle of the night, the Jeep was rocked by something that bumped hard against it side. The bumping shook the Wagoneer so badly that it caused all three sleepers to "pop" wide awake. Bobby started to speak, but Stubby quickly placed his hand over the boy's mouth.

Doc whispered softly, "Be very quiet and follow me. Be quick about it. We might not have much time to get out of here."

Moving fast, he crawled out of the Jeep's side door. The two little campers were right behind him. When they were standing outside the Wagoneer, they were hidden by the Jeep's shadow.

Stubby whispered, "I think it's a big hippo. It must be trying to stratch its tail by rubbing against the Jeep."

On the moonlight side of the Wagoneer, a big male hippo snorted loudly. Doc spoke softly, "He is scratching, but he sounds a little angry. I do not think that he likes the smell of the Jeep."

Stubby peeked around the front end of the Wagoneer. In the moonlight, he could easily see the hippo. The river horse's wet skin sparkled in the light. As Stubby peeked, once again the hippo started to rub. It seemed as if the river horse might tip the Jeep over onto its side.

Doc reached through the Jeep's front window. He opened the "cubby hole" or glove compartment and pulled out a package of firecrackers. Quickly, he struck a match and lighted the package, then he tossed the lighted package of firecrackers over the Jeep's roof. The firecrackers landed alongside the bull hippo. A moment later, they banged, popped, whistled, and screamed as they flashed and sparkled.

The noise and flashes of fire scared the hippo. He ran back to the river and waded out into the water.

Stubby sighed, then he spoke. "I don't think that hippo will come back, so let's go to bed."

The campers climbed into the Wagoneer, but it was hard for them to go to sleep. The night sounds were not peaceful. Many of the animals did not like the smell of the three friends and their Jeep Wagoneer.

Although they were tired from loss of sleep, the campers were glad when the sun began to appear above the horizon.

When Bobby looked out the Jeep's window, his eyes seemed ready to pop out. In the early morning light, he could clearly see the many fat hippos as they followed their pathways back to the river. It looked as if all of the river horses had spent the night feeding upon the plants that grew along the river's bank.

"How big is a hippo?" Bobby asked. "Are they really big enough to tip the Jeep over?"

"River horses," Stubby explained, "are usually about thirteen feet in length as adults. They are commonly five feet tall and weigh around 3000 pounds. Yes, Bobby, a big male hippo could tip the Jeep."

Stubby kept on speaking. "If we study the living

things God has created—I mean plants and animals —we find that each living organism, almost without exception, has something special to help it live its way of life. Do you know that a hippo can take a deep breath, then close its nose and ear openings? This makes it able to hold its breath for about six minutes. This is the main reason a hippo can stay under water for such a long time. There are places, primarily for tourists, where people can sit in rooms that are below the water and look through glass windows at hippos as they trot along on the bottom of a pond or lake. God made everything. Yes, He made things very good, just as He told us in His Word."

In the early morning light, the three men prayed. They thanked God for helping them at the roadblock, and they thanked Him for protecting them from bad trouble with the hippo.

After prayer time, the men ate breakfast. After eating, it took only a few minutes to clean the pots and pans and pack their things. Minutes later, they slowly drove along a trail on the river's bank. Doc drove the Jeep toward a boat dock.

It was almost noon when the boatman came to the dock. When he arrived, the three friends hired him to pilot them up the Nile River. They hoped to go up river until they were near the foot of Murchison Falls.

As they chugged along in the boat, Stubby pointed to a mother hippo and her baby. The two hippos were standing in the water near the river's edge. Beads of water sparkled as sunlight was reflected from their wet skins.

When the boatman drove close to the two river horses, mother hippo led her baby out of the water.

They watched the boat chug past while standing on the bank.

Suddenly, a big male hippo poked his head out of the water. The hippo roared. It was a sound that made chills and shivers run up and down the backs of the three friends.

A moment after the roaring sound, the big hippo's feet began to churn the water as he swam toward the boat. The angry river horse caused the water to become white with foam as it rapidly moved closer and closer.

Even before he reached the chugging boat, the hippo opened his mouth. When Bobby saw the open mouth, he thought it looked like a cave. To the boy midget the hippo's tusk-like teeth looked like spears.

When the boatman saw the hippo racing through the water, he yelled, "We have to get out of here! A hippo that big could wreck my boat. Hang on! If he catches us, it would be very bad. But I have a couple of surprises waiting for him."

The motor roared as the boatman opened the throttle. The boat began to speed up, but the hippo was swimming even faster. He was getting very close to the boat.

"Mr. Hippo," the boatman shouted, "here comes surprise number one." With a big push, he shoved an empty steel barrel into the water. The barrel landed in the water right right in front of the angry hippopotamus. Although the hippo tried to stop, he crashed into the barrel. The river horse opened his mouth and tried to bite the bouncing barrel, but the bobbing barrel floated away from him. When he charged after the barrel, it kept bobbing out of his reach as it was carried down stream by the river's fast current.

The boatman laughed. He said, "Hippos have chased me before. Now, I always have a couple of empty barrels to fool them. Later, you will have to help me find my barrel. I'll probably need it again someday."

Minute by minute, the Nile River's current was getting stronger. It was becoming very hard for the boat to continue upstream against the rushing, tumbling waters.

Stubby said, "It seems as if the river is angry. It's fighting to keep us away from the falls. Wow! The waterfalls are sure rumbling and grumbling. Maybe it's warning us not to come any closer."

Above the roar of the angry river, the boatman's voice could barely be heard. He shouted, "Murchison Falls is just around the next bend in the river's path. We cannot go much closer. The current is getting too strong. If we go too far, the river gods will get us. They will swallow all of us."

Bobby, Stubby, and Doc all started to talk at once. They told the boatman that there were no "river gods." There is only one God.

Poly poly, the boat fought the rushing water until it made its way around the bend. The three men took pictures of the falls, then the boat was slowly pushed backward down the great Nile River.

Chapter Seventeen

The boat's motor fought against the river's strong current. Struggling hard, it moved forward and rounded the bend. Once it made the turn around the bend, Bobby, Stubby, and Doc could see Murchison Falls. It was a beautiful sight to see. The waters of the Nile River rolled, tumbled, and tossed below the falls. The spray from the falls, when touched by sunlight, formed a wondrously-colored rainbow.

Stubby said, "Isn't it wonderful? God made people so they can see colors. He created many colored things for us to see. He made flowers, butterflies, birds, rainbows, and even some snakes with patterns of color. I don't believe any other of His living creations sees colors like we do. What a glorious God we have."

When the boat rounded the bend in the river, it was no longer protected from the great rush of water by the curve in the river's bank. Although the motor kept fighting hard, the boat was slowly pushed downstream.

The African boatman said, "The river gods are angry. They do not want us to go any closer. If we try to keep going, the angry gods will probably smash my boat into small pieces. If the gods dump us in the river, we will either drown or the crocodiles will get us. The crocodiles seem to work for the river gods."

Bobby smiled, but he was really sad. The tiny boy knew that there was only one God. It made him sad to hear the boatman speak of many gods. He hoped that someday the African boatman would learn about the One and only real Living God.

In the churning waters below the Falls, the boatman kept the "nose" or "bow" of his boat pointed upstream, but he slowed the motor. Now, the boat drifted more rapidly downstream. The river current was so strong that the boatman did not dare turn the boat around until it had been pushed back around the bend. After floating downstream for a few minutes, the boat was turned so that it faced downstream. With the current pushing, it was easy for the boat to chug along.

Stubby gently poked his son, then he pointed to some crocodiles who were sunning themselves on a sandbar. "Wow!" he said, "They really are big ones."

While they were watching, a crocodile stood up and walked toward the water. Bobby said, "I wonder how many feet long that big crocodile really is? I don't want to measure him. With his big mouth, he could easily chop me up and eat me!"

"That crocodile," the boatman said, "is at least fifteen feet long, but there are bigger ones. This river has many crocodiles. If we fell out of the boat, they would probably catch us and tear us into pieces."

Bobby shivered. Crocodiles looked mean and ugly to the young boy. For a moment, he wondered why God had made them. But after thinking for a few seconds, he was sure that "crocs" were important as a part of God's Plan.

A big crocodile walked toward the water. The croc seemed to be looking at a herd of hippos which could be seen wading, swimming, and playing nearby.

Almost silently, the four-legged reptile slid into the river. With hardly a ripple, it disappeared beneath the water's surface.

After the crocodile disappeared, the two little travelers turned to watch the herd of river horses as they floated while they browsed on water plants.

One very young hippo left its mother's side to go play in a patch of water hyacinths. The hyacinth plants were in bloom. The beautiful blossoms added color to the river's surface.

"Look," Stubby said, "at that patch of hyacinths. Is that a log floating near its edge?"

"No!" Bobby shouted, "It is a crocodile. It looks like a log because there are flowers stuck on its back."

A big crocodile had quietly floated to the water's surface. He had come to the top at the edge of the hyacinth patch. The four-legged reptile had several pretty hyacinth flowers on its back.

"I believe," Stubby said, "that crocodile is going to try to catch the young hippo. If you watch carefully, you will see that it is moving closer and closer to that fat little river horse. I think Mr. Crocodile looks so much like a log with those flowers on his back that he has fooled all of the hippos. I'm afraid that the baby hippo has gotten too far from its mother."

Suddenly, the air rumbled as a male hippo roared a warning to the herd! Even before his roar had quit sounding, the male hippo's feet were

churning the water as he swam toward the
crocodile.

When the warning was heard, the mother hippo
swam as fast as she could to save her baby. She
swam so fast that the water became covered with
foam.

Bobby shouted, "Dad, she will never get there in
time! She is too far away! I think little fatty is a
goner!"

The crocodile already had his mouth wide open
before the baby river horse saw him. But just as
the crocodile's mouth snapped shut, the tiny hippo
spun around. The snapping jaws of the crocodile
caused the little hippo to squeal in pain. The croc's
bite almost missed, but it chopped off most of the
young hippo's tail!

Once again, the crocodile's mouth opened wide.
This time the croc was very close to the little
hippo. It would catch the young hippo for sure.
Bobby could hardly keep looking. There were tears
in his eyes.

But just before the crocodile's mouth snapped
shut on the baby hippo, the bull hippo crashed into
the crocodile's side. Like an army tank, the bull
moved between the badly scared baby river horse
and the four-legged reptile. Quickly, the bull hippo
turned to face the crocodile. Now, the hippo's
mouth was open wide, and it was the croc's turn to
swim fast as it tried to save its own life!

Quick as a flash, the crocodile dove beneath the
water's surface! It's tail slapped the water hard as it
dove! It barely got away from the father hippo.

When Bobby saw that the baby hippo was going
to be all right, he jumped up and down because he
was very happy. The tiny boy thought crocodiles

were ugly. He did not want the croc to catch the fat little river horse.

Stubby laughed. "Look," he said, "at our short-tailed fat little hippo. Our baby river horse is so close to his mother that he seems to be stuck to her. I don't think that he will swim very far away from her for a long time. He was lucky, but baby hippo will always have a short tail to remind him of the crocodile's sharp teeth. With a short stubby tail such as he has, maybe the baby hippo's parents will name him Stubby."

After watching the hippos and crocodiles for several minutes, the boat moved on down the river.

Not much later, Stubby spotted a many-colored, four-legged reptile as it stood on the river bank. The animal held its head high above the long grasses. When the little man aimed his finger at the reptile, the boatman turned the boat and steered where Stubby pointed.

Doc asked, "Do you know what it is?" Heads shook as the little men told him their answer, so he explained. "This colorful reptile is a monitor lizard. Although it is a reptile similar to crocodiles, this lizard actually eats crocodile eggs. Already we have killed too many lizards. We kill them because people use their many-colored skin to make fancy pocket books, purses, and belts. By killing the monitor lizards, we have upset God's Plan, so now there are too many crocodiles."

Stubby pointed at the river bank. It seemed to be almost covered with crocodiles. He said, "If people do not stop killing so many monitor lizards, crocodiles will fill the river. It might become so bad that not even hippos will be able to live in the Nile."

The boatman piloted his boat on down the river.
As they chugged along, they spotted the steel
barrel. It took him only a minute or two to pick it
up. After chugging on for a few minutes more, he
drove alongside his dock and tied the boat to a
post.

The two little men and Doc climbed out of the
boat. They stood on the dock while looking up and
down the Nile River.

Stubby said, "If this river could talk, I believe it
would have many stories to tell. There would be
stories about fights between the animals; fights
between the animals and people; fights between
people and the river's strong current; as well as
many stories about things that happened which
were good. It could tell about how mankind has
used it as a waterway to carry merchandise and
supplies in boats, canoes, and on rafts. In some
places, the Nile River has been like a highway or
road for transporting things and people from inland
places to the sea coast. Yes, the Nile is an
important waterway, and it has been important for
many years. It would have many exciting stories if
it could talk."

"It seems to me," Bobby said, "that rivers, all
over the world, are often used as if they were roads
made of water."

With a grin on his face, Stubby said, "General,
what are your orders? Shall we go directly to the
Jeep?"

"Yes," Doc answered, "return on the double."
There was laughter in his voice.

Bobby asked, "If you are a 'general,' Doc, what
does that make me? Am I a 'private'?"

Doc laughed and explained. "Bobby," he said,

"you know that I am not a real army general. It is an honorary title. Abdi and his rangers called me 'general' because I helped them in their battles against poachers. It is a never-ending battle. The title has indeed been an honor."

Bobby clicked his heels together and saluted, then the three friends laughed as they started toward the Jeep.

It was several hundred yards from the dock to the Jeep. The three men had almost reached their camping spot when Stubby looked back over his shoulder. "Doc," he said, "we have visitors. Take a look behind us. Just look. Don't turn around."

When Doc looked back, he saw a group of soldiers coming out of the woods. They were wearing army uniforms. The squad of soldiers went out on the dock and talked to the boatman. There was a loud argument, then a gunshot cracked, and the sound of the soldiers laughing could be heard.

Doc softly said, "It is only a few more steps to the Jeep, do not turn around. Remember, the people of this country show great dislike and disgust for any person who shows fear. If we have strength enough not to seem afraid, they might leave us alone. Giving them our things would do no good. If they took them, they would have to kill us. There could be no witnesses left alive!"

Three prayers shot straight from the hearts of Bobby, Stubby, and Doc. The prayers were messages to Lord Jesus. Each message asked for His help.

As he walked toward the Jeep. Bobby wondered if the soldiers had shot the boatman. He held back the tears even though he was afraid. The tiny boy could almost feel that the army men were

watching. He tried hard to keep them from seeing
that he was afraid.

When they reached the Jeep, Doc thought about
jumping in and driving away, but the only road out
went back past the dock and the soldiers. There
was no way that they could drive past the army
men safely. If they tried, it would be easy for
machine gun bullets and rifle shots to stop them.

"Bobby," Doc whispered, "get into the Jeep.
Crawl up on the bed and stay there unless they ask
you to come out. Stubby, you and I will do as
always when we start on a safari. You pull the
hood release lever and I will check the oil and
radiator. We will carry out our regular jobs. Do
everything slowly. Remember, there may be soldiers
who can speak English, so be careful what you say.
Okay, let's do it."

After Doc had finished checking the oil, he
wiped every light, then he started to clean the
windshield. While Doc cleaned the windshield,
Stubby was also busy.

After he had pulled the hood release lever for
Doc, Stubby hopped out of the Jeep. He walked
around the Wagoneer and checked each tire. When
this work was done, he climbed up on the roof and
checked the ropes that held the camping
equipment in the roof carrier.

Inside the Jeep, Bobby kept praying. He said,
"Lord Jesus, please take care of my Dad and Doc.
I love them and they love me. Dear Jesus, You
know we all love You."

While Stubby checked the ropes that held things
on the carrier, the soldiers were walking toward the
Jeep. As they came toward him, the little man slid
down the Wagoneer's windshield onto its hood.

From there he climbed down to the ground.

His feet had hardly touched the ground when a rifle cracked. The bullet made dirt fly as it hit the ground close to Stubby's feet. Of course, it scared the little man, but he smiled and reached out his tiny hand. He said, "I have taught marksmanship. Put up a target. Perhaps I can teach you, so you can be a marksman. You must learn not to jerk on the trigger. It should be squeezed gently."

Doc watched the soldier's face. He was sure the soldier understood Stubby. A moment later, Doc walked over and stood beside Stubby. He smiled at the squad leader. He read a number from the soldier's shirt, then he stepped closer to the squad leader. In a crisp tone of voice, he said, "Mr. Stevens, write down the leader's number. I do not want to get it wrong. I have met the President of this country. If I see him again I want to tell him about this squad leader."

The little man did as he had been told. He was careful to get the number written correctly. When he had finished, he saluted the squad leader and returned to the Jeep. He stopped in front of Doc. "Sir," he said, "is there anything more you want me to do?"

"No," Doc said, "I think that is all." After his words to Stubby, the gray-haired man saluted the squad leader, then he and Stubby climbed into the Jeep.

The soldiers returned Doc's salute, then they walked along a forest trail. In a few minutes, they were no longer in sight.

As soon as the soldiers were gone, Stubby, Bobby, and Doc drove to the boat dock. It was good to see the boatman kneeling on the floor of his boat. The soldiers had not hurt him, but they had shot a hole in the bottom of his boat. The boatman was trying to fix the hole to keep the water out.

Not long after checking and finding that the boatman had not been hurt, the three Americans waved goodbye to the African and headed along a road that would take them to a famous National Reserve.

On the way to the Reserve, Doc once again carefully explained to Bobby that bravery is a trait East Africans admire. However, there are many peoples of the world who feel it is a special honor to kill a brave person. He said, "Bobby, there is no way a person can be sure that he is doing the right thing when danger is faced, but it is important to know the people and their cultural beliefs. When you know them, it takes away much of the risk. The very best way I know of winning any victory is to study and learn, then seek God's help and have faith."

As the three friends talked, time and miles clicked past. It seemed to be only a short journey to the National Reserve.

When they reached the Reserve entrance, the rangers gave Doc a telegram. The message came from Abdi. It read, "Come home. Big problem. Need help. Hurry!"

It was late afternoon when the Wagoneer arrived at the Reserve. The travelers had planned to camp in the area, but after reading Abdi's message they decided to hurry home.

Doc said, "If we drive through the Reserve and out the other side, we will be on a roadway that leads to home. Abdi needs us so I believe we should keep going during the night." The two little men agreed.

As they were following a trail through the Reserve, Doc pointed to a cluster of big trees. He drove toward the trees. "Perhaps," he said, "we will see lions."

Bobby wasn't very interested. After all, he had seen lots of lions, but as they came near the trees, he turned his head and looked out the Jeep's side window. What he saw almost caused him to fall off the seat. He blinked his eyes to make sure that he was awake. "Holy cow," he said, "there are lions up in that tree. Some of them are sleeping. How did they get up there? Can lions climb trees?"

Stubby laughed. "In this place," he said, "simbas do climb trees. I was told, by my teacher, that they climb to get away from a kind of fly that bites. The fly lives quite close to the ground, so the lions climb high to get away from them. My teacher wants me to tell you that he read it, but he can't prove it. The lions even sleep in the trees." When Stubby looked at Doc, the teacher nodded his head.

Bobby yelled, "Ouch! I think that I should climb up into one of those trees with the lions. A fly bit me and it really does hurt!"

"You had better do some more thinking," Stubby said, "before you climb that tree. It would take many fly bites to be bad, but one lion bite and you would be finished."

Doc laughed. "Yes," he said, "as a Kenyan would say, only one lion bite and you would be 'quisha.' 'Quisha' means 'finished'."

The travelers took pictures of the lions, then the Jeep was headed out of the Reserve. The three

Americans were going to answer Abdi's call for help.

It was a long drive back to Abdi's home. He had told them to hurry. Doc, with Stubby sitting by his side, planned to drive through the night. If all went well, Bobby, Stubby, and Doc would be with Abdi before the sun's rays shone over the Ngong Hills.

Chapter Eighteen

All night long the Jeep raced along the roadways. At times, it bounced along stretches of rough road, but it did not stop except to give Doc time to pour gasoline from a can into the gas tank.

It was nearly four o'clock in the morning when the two tired men and the little boy got back to Nairobi. They had driven many miles without any time to sleep.

Abdi's telegram had asked them to "Hurry." Bobby, Stubby, and Doc had come just as fast as they could.

When the Jeep Wagoneer arrived at Abdi's home, a light was still on in the living room. The Warden had waited up for his friends. He met them at the door. "Jambo, rafiki" he said, "I have been expecting you."

The three travelers smiled. They knew "Jambo, rafiki" meant "hello, friend."

It was easy to see that Abdi was worried, so Doc asked him, "What is wrong? Has something happened to Patience?"

The African Warden shook his head. "Poachers," he said, "have killed another cheetah. They have killed Timid. She returned to the Reserve the day you left. Her four young adults came back with her. As you know, they are not quite old enough to take care of themselves. Those young cats need another two months before they will be able to live alone in the wild country. We have not been able to get close enough to dart them. Doc, we have to dart them. If we can't help them, they will all die."

At first, Doc had fire and anger in his eyes, but when he spoke to his two little friends, his eyes filled with tears. Doc said, "Timid was a daughter of Patience. She was about three years old when she had her first litter of babies. I played with Timid almost from the time she was born, and I played with her cubs several months before I returned to America. This lady cheetah and her cubs were very special friends of mine. It is hard to believe that the golden lady I called 'Timid' is dead. If I can help save her family, I certainly will. But it has been almost a year since I last saw those cheetahs. They were only cubs, now they are almost adults. Will they still remember me?"

"We have to dart them," Abdi repeated. "You, Doc, are our only chance. If we do not catch them, I am sure they will all die."

Abdi told his friends about the scared cheetahs. For three days, he and his rangers had tried to get close enough to the spotted cats to dart them. The cheetahs had always kept too far away. In those three days, the cats had not eaten anything. The African did not know when the young adult cheetahs had last had food. Last night was a very bad time. Lions almost caught two of the motherless cats.

The Warden quit talking. He turned to go to his room. As he walked away, he said, "You had better ask your God for help. Maybe He can help us save one or two of the cheetahs."

Soon everyone was in bed. Bobby, Stubby, and

Doc all prayed for help.

During his sleep, Bobby dreamed. In his dream, the little man was being chased by a lion, so he ran to a tree and climbed high into its branches. The simba could not climb the tree. It must have been a Kenyan lion. As you know, a Ugandan lion would have climbed the tree and gobbled him up. The tiny boy stopped dreaming and rolled over. If you listened, a soft snoring sound could be heard.

Shortly after sunrise, Stubby awakened. Quickly, he got out of bed and dressed. In a few minutes everyone in the house was out of bed. Another day had begun.

Stubby started to make breakfast when the CB radio in Abdi's house began to crackle. A ranger was calling Abdi. The rangers gave the Warden some bad news. It was about Timid's family. During the night, the four cheetahs had been chased by a leopard. Although the cheetahs did get away, they have been chased until they entered lion territory. The rangers had even seen lions as they slept not very far away from the spotted cats. The sleeping lions curled up under a thorn bush.

After the CB report, Abdi said, "There will be no breakfast. If we do not catch those cheetahs, the lions will get them for sure."

The three friends left at once and headed into the wild country. Abdi and Stubby were in the Land Rover while Bobby and Doc came along behind in the yellow Jeep.

Abdi and Doc hoped that Timid's family would remember the yellow Jeep. If the cats remembered, maybe the Wagoneer could get close enough to dart the cheetahs. Even so, Abdi did not believe they would be able to save more than one or two of the spotted cats. He was sure the first shot, from the dart gun, would scare the cheetahs away. At least two of the cats with the tear-streaked faces would run before they could be darted. The runaway cheetahs would surely die.

The African Warden led Doc and Bobby into the wild country. He took them to the spot where the four cheetahs were hiding.

When Doc saw the spotted cats, he could hardly believe his eyes. The cheetahs looked starved and very scared.

Doc said, "You men stay here. Bobby and I will try to drive closer. We will have to wait and see what happens."

The yellow Jeep moved slowly toward the four cheetahs. As it came near, the spotted cats stood up. A moment later, they started to move further away. One of the cheetahs looked back over its shoulder. It seemed to be trying to remember. The cheetah chirped softly. It was calling for help.

At once, Doc stopped the Jeep. He put his head out the window and chirped. All four spotted cats stopped. They turned to look at the yellow Jeep.

Doc whispered to Bobby. He said, "Kimoya, the smallest one, is trying to remember. I think she is the smartest cheetah in the family. If she remembers, the others will follow her."

Once again, the gray-haired man put his head out the Jeep's window and chirped. This time the chirp was a different sound.

Like a lost child who has just found its way home, Kimoya bounced across the bush country as she ran to the Jeep. Her brothers and sisters were close behind her.

Suddenly, the cheetahs stopped. They looked at

the Land Rovers and would not come any closer.

Doc picked up his CB radio. "Abdi," he said, "will you and your rangers please back up? The cheetahs are remembering, but they are afraid of the Rovers. I believe they will come to me, but I must get their trust. It might take a little while before they get over being afraid."

Abdi wondered why the cheetahs were afraid of the Land Rovers. Although he did not understand, he signaled his rangers to move back. The two Rovers moved further away from the Jeep.

This time, when Doc chirped, the cheetahs ran to the Jeep. They jumped on the Wagoneer's hood and scrambled to the roof, then the spotted cats stretched out. The cheetahs felt safe.

Bobby had never seen this family of cheetahs. He turned to speak to Doc. When he saw the gray-haired man, the tiny boy's heart almost stopped and his eyes almost popped out.

Doc was squirming out the Jeep's window. He ended up sitting on the Jeep's window ledge with his arms, head, and shoulders outside while his feet and legs were inside.

A wild cheetah, almost fully grown, lay stretched out on the Wagoneer's roof. It was Kimoya.

Abdi, Stubby, and the rangers sat in their Land Rovers. They stared at the Jeep.

Stubby said, "I can't believe my eyes. Isn't that Doc sitting in the Jeep's window? I think he is playing with those cheetahs."

Abdi smiled. "Doc," he said, "is an unusual man. It is hard to believe, but that family of cheetahs has not forgotten him, although he has been gone for almost a year. They remembered his love for them. It was the one he calls Kimoya who

remembered first. She was always Doc's favorite.
He was her best friend."

Stubby, Abdi, and his rangers started laughing.
Believe it or not, Doc had lifted the tip of Kimoya's
tail. He held the tip of the cat's tail under his nose
to make it look as if he had a moustache.

As the rangers, Abdi, and Stubby watched, Doc
petted, scratched, and pulled ticks and burrs from
the fur of all four spotted cats. The cheetahs
purred to show that they liked it.

As Abdi watched, his smile began to fade away.
The African was thinking about darting the cats.
Darting would hurt the spotted cats, and the loud
bang of the gun always frightened them. Warden
Abdi was sure that Doc would have a hard time
hurting the cheetahs. The white bwana would be
very sad.

After playing with the cheethas for a few
minutes, Doc crawled back through the window
and into the Jeep. He called Abdi on his CB radio.
He said, "I have an idea. Is there any reason why I
can't dart these cats by hand? I mean not use a
gun at all. If I'm careful, I don't think it would hurt
much more than picking ticks."

"Yes," Abdi said, "there is a very good reason.
Listen rafiki, you know as well as I do that darting
hurts a lot more than picking ticks. The chance of
your being bitten badly is great."

Doc laughed. He said, "I guess you will have to
look the other way, my friend, because I want to
try it my way. Have four darts ready for use, I'm
coming after them."

The gray-haired man opened the Jeep's door,
then he stepped outside. He did not stand up
straight. Instead, he almost crawled along. The

cheetahs watched him, but their minds recalled the same picture from the past, so they were not afraid.

Doc crawled to the Warden's Rover where he was given four darts used to make animals go to sleep. He took the darts and crawled back to the Jeep.

When Doc got back to the Jeep, he carefully handed the darts to Bobby. "Now," he said, "my little rafiki, I need your help. You must hold the sleep needles and hand them to me when I put my hand in the window. Give them to me one at a time, please. Try not to touch the needle. It should be kept clean."

The gray-haired man squirmed out the Jeep's window. He sat half in and half out of the Wagoneer with his elbows resting on the roof. Doc scratched the back leg of a cheetah with his fingers, then he carefully poked a needle into its leg. Although the spotted cat's leg jerked, the cheetah did not move away.

Quickly, he put his hand through the Jeep's open window. Very carefully, Bobby gave him another dart. It only took a few minutes to use three darts. Already three cheetahs were getting sleepy. A few minutes longer and they would be fast asleep.

Suddenly, Kimoya sat up and looked across the grasslands. The lady cat had seen a Thompson's gazelle. The spotted cat crawled down from the Wagoneer's roof. First to the hood and then to the ground. The spotted lady was going to try to make a kill.

While Kimoya was sneaking through the grass trying to get close to the gazelle, Abdi drove his Rover and parked alongside the Jeep. He said, "I had to come, Doc. We will have to put those three cats in our cage. They are so sleepy that I was afraid they might fall off the roof and get hurt."

The rangers and Abdi put the three cats in a big cage. The cats were already asleep. A moment later, the Africans drove away.

Kimoya could not get close enough to the gazelle so she did not try to catch it. The young lady cheetah started to go back to the Jeep, but she saw the rangers and Abdi loading her two brothers and her sister into a cage.

The young female cat became frightened. Even when the Land Rovers drove away from the Jeep, the cheetah would not return to the Wagoneer.

Doc chirped and chirped, but the cat with the tear-streaked face would not come to the Jeep.

Bobby saw tears come into Doc's eyes. He asked, "Doc, can we get close enough to dart her? I don't think she trusts us anymore."

The gray-haired man did not answer, but he started the Wagoneer and drove very slowly, poly-poly, over to Abdi's Rover.

"Abdi," Doc said, "I think you should get in here with Bobby and me. Bring your dart gun with you and a couple of spare darts. Somehow we must get close to Kimoya. You will have to shoot her with a dart."

The African Warden got into the Jeep Wagoneer. Very poly-poly the yellow Jeep headed toward the young lady cheetah.

Bobby prayed. He said, "Dear Heavenly Father, help us save the lady cheetah. Kimoya is very beautiful and she is one of Your creations. Help us so we can help her. Amen."

Chapter Nineteen

Three of the four cheetahs had been darted. The darted spotted cats were fast asleep. They were resting in a cage on the back of a Land Rover truck that was being driven by Abdi's rangers.

The fourth young adult cheetah, Kimoya, was sitting on a grass-covered mound. Kimoya was all alone and she was crying. First, her mother had been killed by poachers and now her two brothers and her sister were gone. The lady cheetah cried and cried!

Abdi and Doc were sitting up front in the Jeep, and Bobby had crawled onto the bed in the back of the Wagoneer, as the yellow Jeep rolled across the grasslands. The gray-haired man drove very slowly as he tried to get close to the golden cat.

As the Jeep came near, Kimoya stood up. The cheetah was very lonely and sad, but she was ready to run away.

Doc whispered a prayer. "God, please let her trust me just a little bit. Please let us get close enough to shoot her with the dart gun."

The gray-haired man spoke to Abdi. "Rafiki," he said, "we cannot get much closer. Can you hit her with a dart from here?"

The African shook his head. "No," he said, "it is still too far for my dart gun to reach. If I should miss, I do not believe there will be a second chance. Kimoya would run so far away into that rough country that we would never get her out. We have to get closer."

Foot by foot, yard after yard, the Jeep moved closer to Kimoya.

A few minutes later, Abdi whispered to Doc. "You can stop now," he said. "I am close enough, if she doesn't move, my dart gun can reach the cheetah from here."

The black African carefully aimed his dart gun. When he squeezed the trigger, the gun banged loudly. The dart hit Kimoya and the needle stuck in the fat part of the lady cheetah's back leg. Although Abdi had made a good shot, the drug does not cause sleep at once, so Kimoya started to run toward the rough and rocky country.

Doc pushed hard on the gas pedal. He drove the Jeep in a circular path as he raced to get in front of Kimoya. The lady cheetah was running toward a thorn bush-covered area.

Bobby screamed, "A lion is coming out of those bushes. It is coming toward Kimoya."

A quick shift of gears by Doc and the Jeep shot forward. Doc headed straight at the lion. If he could help it, no simba was going to kill the young lady cheetah.

As the Wagoneer raced ahead, the gray-haired man kept tooting the horn. The roaring motor, loud horn, and big cloud of dust caused by the Jeep scared the simba. The lion turned and ran back into the bushes.

Although the drug from the dart was making her sleepy, Kimoya saw the lion. She stopped running and stumbled toward the Jeep. Only a few steps were taken, then she flopped to the ground.

Doc pushed the brakes hard and the Wagoneer slid to a stop. He opened the door and jumped out. The gray-haired man ran to the cheetah and sat down beside her. He held Kimoya's head in his lap and gently scratched the lady cheetah's ears and neck until she quit crying. Finally, the drug put the spotted cat to sleep.

Abdi walked over to where Doc held Kimoya. The two men carried her to the cage and gently placed her inside. The four cheetahs were safe. When Stubby looked for the rangers, they were standing in a circle with their backs toward the circle's center. Their rifles were in the ready position. The rangers kept watching the bushes in all directions. If a lion were to come after their friend Doc, they would kill it! The rifles were not dart guns, but high-powered hunting guns.

Shortly after Kimoya was placed in a cage, the rangers took the four almost grown cheetahs back to Abdi's house. They put the sleeping cats in a big pen and sat down to wait for them to awaken.

When the cheetahs were fully awake, an impala was turned loose in the pen. The four cheetahs make a quick kill.

A ranger told Bobby that the impala had a crippled leg. It could not have lived long in the wild country.

Bobby smiled. He remembered the words "some must die that others might live." The young boy was sure God's Plan was working.

Late in the afternoon, Stubby stood looking out a window at Abdi's house. He was watching the setting sun's golden rays over the grasslands. It made a beautiful picture, but it had been a very sad day. It was great that all four cheetahs had

been saved and the poachers who had killed Timid
were caught, but catching the illegal hunters did
not make Stubby happy. He knew that the really
bad people were those who bought the spotted cat
skins. Poaching would soon stop if the skin buyers
could be arrested and punished. But almost always
the skin buyers were not caught.

When night came, the four friends went to bed
early. The men needed to catch up on their sleep.
After driving all night and darting the cheetahs
during the day, the three Americans were very tired.

In their prayers, Stubby and Bobby asked God to
help all people learn to love their neighbors and to
love all His creations. Stubby said, "Lord Jesus help
save the cheetahs. Already they are almost all
gone. Amen."

It was a bright night with a full moon shining in
an almost cloudless sky. If you were to look out
the windows of Stubby's bedroom, the pen holding
the cheetahs was easily seen.

As Stubby lay in bed, he watched the four
spotted cats as they walked back and forth along
the pen's high fence. His tiny ears could also hear
the constant chirping of the cheetahs. Although the
cats were nearly old enough to leave their mother
and live alone, they still cried for her.

Stubby sat up in bed. He stared out the window
at the cheetahs. "That's it," he said to himself,
"that is why Doc calls them golden cats. When
they stand in the moonlight, those cats do look like
statues made of gold." He rolled over and went to
sleep.

Long after Bobby, Stubby, and Abdi had gone to
sleep, Doc lay awake. He kept listening to the
chirping cries of the four cheetahs. It made him sad

to hear the golden cats cry for their mother. With their sad crying, Doc knew he could not sleep, so he got out of bed and quietly dressed. Almost silently, he walked down a hallway and opened the back door. He left the house and walked to the cheetah pen.

When the four cheetahs saw Doc coming, they stopped crying. Four pairs of cat eyes watched the gray-haired man as he opened the pen's gate and entered. The cheetahs kept watching as Doc closed the gate and locked it, then sat down with his back leaning against the fence. A moment later, he chirped softly.

The four cheetahs listened to Doc, then the lady cheetah, Kimoya, came to stand at his side.

A white hand reached out to her. Fingers gently scratched the golden lady's head and chin. Kimoya flopped down and placed her head in Doc's lap.

In a short time the other three cheetahs came to Doc's side. It was only a few minutes before they were all fast asleep. Through the night and early morning hours, the cats and Doc slept. The cheetahs no longer cried. The only sounds that could be heard were the purring cats and the snoring of Doc.

Abdi awakened before dawn. He got out of bed and dressed quietly, then he peeked in Stubby's and Bobby's room. Both little men were sleeping, so he walked down the hallway that led to Doc's room. As he passed the hall clock, the African remembered the fight with the spitting cobra and how it had nearly killed the gray-haired man. When he reached Doc's room and looked inside, the bed was empty. Abdi could not understand it. He could see the bathroom was also empty. What had happened to Doc? Where was his dear rafiki?

Quickly the African walked to the front door and stepped outside. He stood on the porch while his eyes searched across the grasslands. Although the sun was still below the horizon, the flush of dawn made it easy to see, but he could not see his friend.

A thought came to Abdi's mind and a smile covered his black face as he hurried around to the back of the house and headed for the cheetah pen, but he soon stopped. The African could see his friend. He did not speak to Doc, but very quietly the black man trotted back to the house and went into the room where Stubby and Bobby slept.

Quickly, he awakened the two little men and signaled for them to quietly follow him to the cheetah pen.

When the two little men and Abdi got to the pen, Doc was still asleep. Kimoya, Doc's favorite cheetah, had her head on his lap and the other cheetahs were pressed against his sides and legs.

Kimoya sat up to stare at the three men visitors. When she moved Doc awakened. "Well," he stammered, "they were crying and very lonesome and they badly needed sleep, so I came out to keep them company. I really didn't have anything better to do. After all, their crying was keeping me awake." Everyone laughed.

"Someday," Bobby said, "I hope animals learn to love me."

Stubby spoke. "Son," he said, "I shouldn't have to remind you. Animals do love you. Have you forgotten Silver Tip and the ponies back at Mountain Haven?"

That morning while the men were eating

breakfast, Bobby asked, "Doc, how did you learn so much about cheetahs?"

"From Mr. Ben, Mr. Abdi, and Timid," Doc said. "They taught me. You know Abdi, and maybe someday you will meet Mr. Ben. He is a wonderful person. I think you would like him."

Abdi nodded his head. He agreed with Doc.

THE END